"I'M TRYING TO FIGURE OUT WHAT IT IS ABOUT YOU that yanks my chain. I don't trust you. I'm not sure I like you. You remind me too much of myself, Jessie. You've got an edge."

"My name is Jessica. Try to remember that. Now move . . . before I cut your heart out."

That slow smile she was beginning to recognize eased over his face. "Too late for that. I don't have a heart."

"Then I'll aim lower."

"Jessie, girl, you've got a wicked mouth," he said.

"Is that a crime?" Her voice came out no more than a bedroom whisper. Her lips felt dry but she didn't dare wet them with her tongue. That would be an invitation to disaster, an invitation to be kissed.

As Sully lowered his head, she realized her mistake. Men like Sully never waited for invitations. "Darlin' "—his lips were almost on hers— "the only crime would be letting a mouth like yours go to waste. . . ."

WHAT ARE *LOVESWEPT* ROMANCES?

They are stories of true romance and touching emotion. We believe those two very important ingredients are constants in our highly sensual and very believable stories in the LOVESWEPT line. Our goal is to give you, the reader, stories of consistently high quality that may sometimes make you laugh, sometimes make you cry, but are always fresh and creative and contain many delightful surprises within their pages.

Most romance fans read an enormous number of books. Those they truly love, they keep. Others may be traded with friends and soon forgotten. We hope that each LOVE-SWEPT romance will be a treasure—a "keeper." We will always try to publish

LOVE STORIES YOU'LL NEVER FORGET BY AUTHORS YOU'LL ALWAYS REMEMBER

The Editors

Loveswept® 774

BAD TO THE BONE

DEBRA DIXON

BANTAM BOOKS
NEW YORK · TORONTO · LONDON · SYDNEY · AUCKLAND

BAD TO THE BONE

A Bantam Book / February 1996

ISBN 0-553-44500-6

Published simultaneously in the United States and Canada

Bantam Books *are published by Bantam Books, a division of Bantam Dou-*
bleday Dell Publishing Group, Inc. Its trademark, consisting of the words
"Bantam Books" and the portrayal of a rooster, is Registered in U.S.
Patent and Trademark Office and in other countries. Marca Registrada.
Bantam Books, 1540 Broadway, New York, New York 10036.

PRINTED IN THE UNITED STATES OF AMERICA

OPM   0 9 8 7 6 5 4 3 2 1

For Shauna Summers—
because she "gets" it

AUTHOR'S NOTE

Literary license is a wonderful thing. It's like permission to be wild. Why am I telling you this? Because I've taken a little license. *Okay, Okay!* I'll confess. I've taken a lot, but I have wanted to shake up a fairy tale from the moment I read the first Loveswept *Treasured Tale.* I wanted to do something on the edge, wanted to stand my fairy tale on its head and spin it in a new direction.

After all, I thought, my editor didn't bat an eye at the psychic archaeologist and the midwife. She calmly accepted the idea about the ex-navy SEAL and the ice-skating nun. Maybe she'd actually let me go a little farther out on that limb I seem so fond of.

And so it was that I called my editor one fine day.

"I have this idea for *Treasured Tales.* Are you ready for this? It's Goldilocks and the Three Hit Men!"

Upon hearing my clever description, all she could manage was, "Excuse me?"

Encouraged—it doesn't take much to encourage me—I forged ahead. "This isn't going to be an ordinary fairy tale."

"Fairy tales aren't *supposed* to be ordinary."

"My point exactly!" I agreed, so relieved she understood. Then I told her, "There is something that appeals to me about innocence surrounded by predators. My Goldilocks isn't lost in the woods, *but* she is alone and searching. And, of course, the bears have guns in my version."

My very brave editor said, "Scoot over," and joined me on that limb. Isn't that what fairy tales are really all about?

Debra Dixon

PROLOGUE

She forced herself to stay awake in the relentless dark, clinging to a slim hope, a simple plan. Her sense of time had vanished days before. But she could still tell night from day. Night felt different, colder.

That's when *he* came. Always the same routine. He'd open the door, angle the flashlight beam at her, and throw down a sandwich in a Baggie and a carton of milk or juice. Then he'd close the door, leaving her alone in the total blackness of the small damp basement. All without a word.

Except when he—

Automatically shutting off the memory, she realized the whole nightmare would forever be divided not into days or nights, but into the time *before* he killed Jenny and the time *after* he killed Jenny. He'd kill her too. Maybe not tonight, but soon. No one was going to save her. No one was coming for her. She didn't expect them to. Now that Jenny was gone, she was completely alone.

Shivering against the cold and the fear and the aching loss, she lay on a bare mattress that smelled of mold and something worse she couldn't name. Anxiously she raised herself to a sitting position and pulled back the corner of the mattress. A little sigh escaped her as she felt carefully with her hand, reassuring herself for the hundredth time that it was still there. She hadn't dreamed it.

The long shard of glass was dagger shaped with a wicked point. She had found it in the corner where it must have fallen when someone pulled out the window and bricked in the opening. Her fingertips brushed softly against the cool glass, remembering how it had been half buried in loose dirt, a treasure waiting to be discovered. That's when the idea had come to her; that's when she had decided to try.

Outside she heard the faint rumble of an engine. Fighting sudden nausea, she clutched her uneasy stomach through her T-shirt. Her heart pumped the sick feeling through her body with every erratic beat. When dread threatened her resolve, she forced herself to grab the long, sharp wedge of glass. She had to be ready before he came. She might not get another chance.

Terrified, she walked to the rickety wooden stairs which jutted out into the room and started up them. *One, two, three, four. . . .*

She counted the steps as she climbed; she'd counted them a thousand times that day. Practiced crouching and balancing on top of the flat guardrail at the landing until her back ached and her legs screamed. But not with the piece of glass. That had been too precious to risk. Even now she was more terrified of breaking the only weapon she had than she was of what lay ahead.

As silently as she could, she crawled onto the railing, choosing the side nearest the door hinges. Clumsily she wobbled on her hands and knees, unable to get to her feet, her nerves interfering with her balance. When she couldn't stop shaking, she began to panic, which only made the shaking worse.

She had to stand up. Her hands had to be free. The door had to swing all the way open without touching her. Otherwise he'd know she was waiting, and she'd lose her chance. Closing her eyes, she tried to calm herself. This railing was just like the balance beams she had made last summer, she told herself. Just an old two-by-four supported by volumes "A" and "M" of the encyclopedia. She wet her lips and tried again. This time she made it.

With the glass held gingerly in one hand, she tried not to think about the floor below or her chances of surviving a fall like that. It didn't matter. He was going to kill her anyway. He had killed Jenny just to make a point. She had no choice. Quickly she pulled a torn strip of T-shirt from her pocket and wrapped the wide end of the glass. She wrapped a second strip around her hand.

Beyond the door she could hear muffled noise. Maybe the sound of a paper sack, a chair dragging across a floor. But no footsteps.

Why didn't he come?

Sweat trickled down her temple and the back of her neck. Finally she could hear the thud of boots as he walked toward the door.

One by one, four dead bolts clicked, and the knob turned. She held her breath, afraid the tiniest sound would give her away. The door swung gently open, the edge of it bouncing against the railing in front of her sneaker. Light flashed down the stairs, arrowing toward the mattress.

Please, she begged silently, adjusting her grip on the glass-knife. *One more step. So I can see you. Please!*

He took the step.

In one action she made herself drive the glass into the side of his throat and tried to shove him down the stairs. She shuddered at the feel of the glass as it slid home, but she couldn't allow herself to pity him. Not if she wanted to survive.

Half-turning, he grabbed for her. She screamed and lunged for the door—clinging to it, fighting for balance as she kicked him hard enough to send him plunging down the stairs. Without wasting a second, she jumped to the landing and got around the door, frantically pulling it shut and locking the bolts.

She ran out into the night, feeling almost safe for the first time; until she realized she was in the middle of nowhere. There were no neighbors, no traffic on the road, no one to save her. Then she saw a hint of light through the trees in the distance. She didn't stop running or screaming for help until an old man came bolting out of a country home and into the yard in front of her. He was barefoot and wearing pajamas, but he had a shotgun. "Hey now! Who are you running from? What's this about?"

"Please," was all she could get out as she reached him. The words stuck in her throat.

He grabbed hold of her arm to steady her, then tilted her chin up to the moonlight so he could look down into her face. "Oh, my God. You're one of those little girls they're looking for. One of the twins." He pushed her behind him, backing her toward the safety of his house.

Little girls? Jessie Dannemora almost laughed.

ONE

Sometimes Jessica would go months without the nightmare, and then she'd have it every night for a week. Always the same. Always the feeling of helplessness and terror. Always the scream that sliced through her heart and woke her—the scream no one else could hear because it was in her mind. It was Jenny's scream —sharp and clear after all these years.

Midnight had come and gone, but Jessica still huddled in the corner of her sofa, wrapped in an old starburst quilt and staring at a dark television screen. She shouldn't have needed the quilt; Utopia, Texas, was warm in June. Unfortunately, the chill came from inside herself—from the fear of going to sleep and confronting the past again.

This had been a bad week.

Who was she kidding? This had been a bad year.

The phone rang twice before the sound of the bell penetrated her reverie. The telephone didn't ring often. When it did, Jessica never answered until her machine screened the call. All the same, as if compelled, her hand snaked out from beneath the quilt and snagged the receiver.

"What?" Her less than cordial greeting clearly flustered the caller.

Silence reigned for a second, and she thought they'd hung up until she heard an unmistakably young female voice say, "M-miss Dannemora?"

Jessica threw off the quilt and sat up as a shiver slid along her spine, distributing alarm until the hair on the back of her neck stood up. No one was supposed to know how to find Jessica Dannemora. *No one.*

Except Phil.

She'd become Jessica Daniels years ago. That was part of the deal. No one knew the nature of their association; no one else had ever contacted her.

"Who the hell are you?" she asked quietly.

"Iris Munro."

"Iris . . . *Munro.*"

"Yes, ma'am." Her tone was respectful, almost fearful. "Phillip Munro is my father."

"I see." But Jessica didn't see, not at all. This little girl should have been in bed asleep instead of calling her. No one should be calling her. Not anymore. "What do you want?"

"I need to hire you."

Stunned, Jessica tried to find her voice and couldn't. This obscene parody of her conversations with Phil cut sharply into emotional wounds that had only just begun to heal. She didn't need this. She didn't need to be reminded of what she was. Especially not by an innocent child with a shaky voice.

"How old are you?" Jessica finally managed.

"Twelve." There was the briefest pause, and then the girl forged on. "Look, Ms. Dannemora, I wouldn't ask if it wasn't important. I know you're retired. I know your file—"

Jessica's mind reeled. File? Phil had a file on her? There wasn't supposed to be a file. There wasn't supposed to be a record of any kind except her name and number in a little black book.

"—your file says no women and children but this is different," Iris assured her. "You're the only one who can do it."

"It's never different," she told the girl coldly. Then the black sense of humor, which had plagued her all her life, threatened to surface. *Thank you for your confidence, Miss Munro, but I don't kill people anymore. Not for the government. Not for your daddy. Not for you.* It was also the truth, but she couldn't bring herself to believe the child really wanted someone dead.

Except—

Iris had read about her in a file. The girl knew her real name, about the retirement, and how to find her. She was Phil Munro's *daughter*. Conscience reminded Jessica that she'd hardly been any older than Iris when—

Suddenly another explanation occurred to her. Making no effort to hide her disapproval or sarcasm, Jessica said, "I can't believe Phil has stooped so low that he'd send a child to do his dirty work. You tell him that the answer is still no. It will always be no. I don't work anymore."

"Daddy doesn't know I want to hire you."

"He will soon enough," Jessica told her grimly. "Put him on the phone."

"I can't. I don't know where he is. That's why I need you."

Closing her eyes, Jessica tried to tell herself this wasn't her problem. Then Iris made it her problem.

"I think . . . I think something bad has happened to him. And I don't have anyone else."

If Iris had called another night, maybe Jessica could have refused, but not tonight. Not when she remembered so clearly how it felt to be twelve years old, alone and afraid. Not when the pain of Jenny's death was so close to the surface. Quietly Jessica began to ask questions and make plans.

For a second Detective Sullivan Kincaid thought he had the wrong house. It was possible. He was still feeling his way around Jericho—getting used to the island's Gulf breeze and the idea that a rash of car stereo thefts would constitute a crime wave. After double-checking his list of addresses, he got out of the car, satisfied he hadn't made a mistake.

From the street everything looked normal. There were no badly painted signs of upraised palms, crystal balls, or seductive gypsy women. There was nothing which indicated a psychic parlor until he stepped onto the porch.

"Welcome to Jericho," Sully said under his breath as he stared at the array of doorbells.

Oh, they were all for the same occupant, but the trick seemed to be in the selection. Each was clearly marked with a small engraved plate screwed into the siding. Obviously, the visitor was supposed to ring the one that met his needs.

The first buzzer, set with a cat's-eye stone, was for seekers of wealth and beauty. Someone searching for healing, love, or wisdom was urged to press the jade button. A quartz crystal looked like the ticket for those attempting projection on an astral plane.

Sully smiled at the next one. The simple black onyx

button offered protection from evil. Well, hell! What a shame no one ever told him a stone was all he needed. It was too late now. The damage had been done for a long time.

The last bell—turquoise—was for courage.

Five choices.

And not a damn one of them said: BURNED-OUT DETECTIVES LOOKING FOR PSYCHIC TIPSTERS. Well, he'd just have to wing it. Sully decided on turquoise and pushed the buzzer. He needed a little courage if he was going to have to spend another interview in the dark, choking on incense, and snapping the subject out of hokey impromptu trances with spirit guides.

For a nanosecond, Sully almost missed real crime. Then he came to his senses, forcing the restless part of himself back into the corner of his soul where he kept the darkness. Walking away from Houston's major case squad was the first sane decision he'd made in a long time. This was going to be the year of the kinder, gentler Sullivan Kincaid. If it killed him.

When the door opened, Sully frowned. This psychic was older—maybe sixty—and definitely a cut above the rest. Slim and well-dressed in black, she looked like Jericho Island's "psychic to the wealthy." Her hair was a blue-white, close-cropped with a natural wave.

Around her neck was a commanding silver-and-turquoise necklace. The turquoise stone motif repeated in her bracelets and rings. He suspected she'd have decked herself out in jade if he'd pushed that button.

"I'm Lillian Anderson," she said without extending her hand. "I knew you were coming."

"I imagine so, ma'am. I rang the doorbell."

"Yes. But you rang the wrong one."

Sully laughed in spite of himself as he showed her his identification. "I did?"

"Don't worry." She stepped back and ushered him inside. "It's not your fault, Detective."

"No?"

"I don't have a bell for inner peace."

That wiped the smile off Sully's face before he realized it was only a lucky guess from a clever pro. He admired her irony, though—a peace officer without peace. Nice touch.

When she closed the door, she led the way into a modern living room with a stained glass panel-screen shielding one corner. A mythical dragon fought its way across the sections, fire roaring from its mouth.

"I was expecting you," she told him, "because Georgia Petrovich called. You interviewed her this morning, and—it seems—every other palmist, card reader, and psychic on the island."

"Yes, ma'am, that I have." *And I've got the incense headache to prove it.* "I'm trying to locate a psychic who may be able to help us in an investigation."

"I see."

Behind the screen was a small oak table with claw feet. One shelving unit was filled with a dragon collection, the other with crystals, geodes, and gem stones. He was pleasantly surprised to find there wasn't a crystal ball in sight. Lillian sat down across from him and reached for a silk-wrapped rectangle, which rested at the center of the table.

As she undid the ribbon and fished a deck of tarot cards from the silk, she asked, "I hope you don't mind if I shuffle while we talk? The cards help me concentrate."

He shrugged. Anything was better than another incense assault.

"Good," she said. "Now, ask me your questions about this psychic. What has she done to draw the hunter?"

"Excuse me?"

"You pursue her." Lillian casually flipped a couple of cards onto the table in an east-west arrangement, and shuffled again. "Doesn't that make you a hunter?"

Sully glanced at the cards, noticing the gilded edges and rich detail. These weren't mass-produced like the others he'd seen today. No, like the woman who handled them, they looked old and felt real. That bothered him. She was too good at probing weak spots.

Ignoring her question, Sully verified her personal information and background before he finally asked, "Do you practice your . . . art under any other pseudonyms?"

"Like Madame Evangeline?" She smiled. "Georgia told me. No, I don't."

"Have you ever used the name?"

"No."

She added two more cards to complete the compass points. This time raising her eyebrow in concern as the cards fell. Sully didn't take the bait, although she wiggled the hook better than most of the psychics he'd visited that day. Instead he asked, "Do you know anyone in the business who goes by that name?"

"No."

"Maybe someone retired or even an amateur who dabbles in the occult?"

"No." She placed one card in the center of the others and set the deck aside. Looking him in the eye, she asked, "Have you considered the possibility that Madame Evangeline doesn't exist on the physical plane?"

Sully's lips twitched, and he had to contemplate the toe of his cowboy boots. "Can't say that I have. She did use the telephone to contact us."

"Perhaps she called from the spirit world. I could try and reach her."

"I don't think that'll be necessary just yet, but I appreciate the offer and your time."

Sully got up to leave. He'd had all the New Age babble he could take for one day. Even when they looked normal, they were living in an alternate universe. At least this one hadn't warned him in hushed, dramatic tones about his dark "aura." Now *that* was a psychic news flash.

"You never did say what this psychic wanted, Detective."

Since his chief wanted Phillip Munro's name kept out of the interviews, Sully said, "She thinks someone might be in danger. We're just trying to check it out, but she didn't leave her phone number last night." He pulled a business card out of his wallet. "If you remember anything, give me a call."

Lillian took the card. As he turned away she whispered, "It won't help."

"Excuse me?" Sully wheeled back around.

"Running from the past that consumes you."

Raising a skeptical brow, he asked, "Is this the part where you talk about my dark aura?"

Lillian shook her head with a tolerant smile. "Georgia sees auras, not me."

"Oh? And what do you see?"

"The occasional angel." She paused a half beat as if debating with herself. Then she added, "Yours is weeping."

Jessica's doubts about coming to Jericho Island multiplied the moment she pulled the rental car into the cul-de-sac. Who called the police? She told Iris to sit tight, say nothing, and wait for her arrival. So what the hell had gone wrong?

"Everything obviously."

She sighed as she looked at the bubble light on the dash of the unmarked police car parked in front of the high-security wall around Munro's beach house. Slowing, she turned into an adjacent driveway and reversed directions. The next block over, she pulled to the side. Now what? If Phil Munro was truly missing as Iris claimed, the last thing she needed was the involvement of bumbling backwater cops.

Jessica swore softly. Leaning back against the headrest, she considered going home to Utopia. She would have except for three things: The little black book, the damned file, and a scared little girl who needed her. No one had needed Jessica in a long time. No one had believed in Jessica for a long time. She couldn't walk away.

Resigned, Jessica picked up the mobile phone she'd gotten when she rented the sedan. The piece of paper with Iris's phone number and address was on the passenger seat, sandwiched between her purse and the map. She checked the number and dialed.

Before the phone could ring a second time, it was snatched up. "The Munro residence!"

"Iris?"

"Aunt Jessica! A policeman just got here. He wants to talk to Daddy. Are you lost again?"

Aunt Jessica? Are you lost again? Iris had struck her as many things during the phone call last night, but stupid was not one of them.

"Yes, honey. I'm on—" Jessica grabbed for the

map, which was neatly folded to this section of the island, and said the first street name she could make out. "I'm on Chandler. How far away is that?"

"Five minutes." Iris gave her directions, which Jessica pretended to be writing down, and the code to the gate. Then the girl whispered a quick good-bye and broke the connection.

Jessica pulled the phone away from her ear and whispered, "Congratulations, Jessie . . . you're an aunt."

It was supposed to be a joke, but it didn't come out that way. Her voice caught in the middle. Those were words she had never expected to hear. Or deserved to hear.

As Iris Munro hung up the phone, Sully decided the setting around her—pastel colors and expensive bleached wood—was the perfect complement for a drop-dead blonde. Little Iris was definitely going to be one of those. Right now she was Goldilocks with Elizabeth Taylor eyes that were much too serious. She wore short faded overalls and a green T-shirt. Only one of the straps was fastened. He wasn't sure if it was a statement or an omission.

"Well, that was my aunt," Iris explained unnecessarily as she fell gracefully back into the profusion of cushions on the white sofa. Her feet, encased in clunky combat boots, looked too big for the rest of her. "I *told* you she was coming. She'll be here soon. You can wait if you want."

"Thanks."

Iris brightened suddenly. "Unless you want to leave your card? I can have her call you tomorrow."

"That's okay. I think I'll wait."

Iris shrugged. "Whatever."

Sully fought laughter. The kid already had the I'm-a-teenager-I-could-care-less look nailed.

Taking a seat in one of the pale-blue-and-white-striped chairs across from the couch, Sully loosened his tie. Thank God the aunt was on her way. His questions would only have alarmed Phil Munro's daughter. She might talk tough, but she was still a little girl. The aunt would be better. It had been one helluva day, and he was ready for it to be over.

More than ready.

If Munro had returned *any* of his calls, Sully would have closed the case, cursed his new chief for sending him on a wild-goose chase, and happily gone home to his wood shop. Turning a few more spindles for his chair backs was preferable to sitting here with the sick feeling he'd stumbled into bad news. Yessiree, buddy. One brief phone conversation with Munro, and he could have been knee-deep in sawdust right now instead of knee-deep in suspicion.

Sully tugged his fingers through his hair, smiled at the kid and hoped his instincts were wrong for once. The odds were against it. Munro couldn't be reached, and no one knew where he was—not his secretary, his vice president, his pilot, or his daughter. Wherever the man was, he wasn't on a scheduled business trip or a family vacation. The man's associates agreed it wasn't unusual for Munro to disappear for a few days, but Sully didn't like coincidences. Not even ones as far-fetched as a psychic warning about an incommunicado executive.

Iris heard the gate buzzer before he did and bounced off the couch. "She's here!"

Although Sully had a good view of the foyer, he stood up and moved closer. The butler, who had been hovering in the hallway, halted Iris with a hand on her arm and went to let in the aunt. He checked the peephole first and then cracked the door. Sully figured he was more bodyguard than butler.

"Aunt Jessica!" Iris went flying toward her, barreling into her and sending the woman back a step. "I'm so glad you're going to stay while Daddy's gone!"

Sully didn't move. Other than to close his mouth.

He had imagined a blonde. He had expected pretty. Rich women could usually manage pretty, and he could usually manage them. He'd had plenty of practice; Houston had more than its share of rich, attractive women who liked to flirt with danger.

So much for expectations.

Aunt Jessica was a sensual brunette whose genetic makeup could just as easily have been Italian as Spanish. The woman wore simple and very short khaki shorts, a red silk T-shirt, and running shoes. Her legs were a shade longer than the Texas legal limit and had probably caused more than one bar brawl—assuming she frequented bars.

Instinct told Sully she'd seen the inside of one or two. She didn't have the look of an ivory tower princess. This was a woman who could call a spade a spade and bring a man to his knees. In fact, most men would be perfectly happy to hit their knees in front of that body. Sully wondered how many already had.

Nothing about her dovetailed with his expectations of Phil Munro's sister. And then there was the startling white streak in her long dark hair, and the way she reacted to her niece. She patted the girl awkwardly on the shoulders as if unsure of how to hug the kid. Finally she set Iris away and turned to the butler. "Would you get my bags out of the car?"

"Yes, *ma'am*."

Sully's eyebrow rose at the sarcasm in the man's tone. He wasn't certain if the distaste was for the woman or for the task. Iris volunteered to help with the bags, and suddenly they were left alone. When Aunt Jessica looked at him for the first time, Sully added dangerous to the list of things he hadn't expected.

Trouble had arrived in Jericho.

TWO

What the hell have you gotten yourself into? Jessica asked herself as she stared into the most unforgiving pair of blue eyes she'd ever seen. The man didn't like her, and he didn't even know her. Smart man, she decided.

As she returned his gaze her sixth sense about danger prodded insistently. *Be very careful with this one, Jessie.* This was no ordinary small-town cop. He'd assessed her too quickly, too subtly. Too completely. She hadn't been taken apart like that in a long time.

Something about him made her feel pressured and on edge—like he had all the answers, and it was time for a pop quiz. Fortunately for Jessica, she'd never met a pop quiz she couldn't ace. She was very good at deflection.

Forcing herself forward, she extended her hand. "Jessica Daniels. And you are?"

He shook her hand, letting the gesture linger a second too long before he pulled a badge out of the hip pocket of his jeans. "Detective Sullivan Kincaid."

As he said his name, Kincaid's deep, confident voice stroked her body as surely as a physical touch.

Like the handshake, his words lingered. They were almost a challenge, tossed out in the same effortless motion that he used to flip open his identification. After a cursory glance at the badge, she took her time inventorying the rest of him—from the askew tie and rolled-up shirtsleeves, all the way down to the well-worn jeans and expensive cowboy boots. She hated to admit it, but the man wore an "attitude" well. And he knew it. He probably counted on it.

Irrationally she felt the need to prick his ego. Or maybe it was the need to establish ground rules and put a little distance between them before Mother Nature's pheromone war got out of hand. The only smart decision was to send the man merrily on his way as quickly as possible.

"Detective Kincaid, it's a good thing you carry that badge."

"Why's that?"

"Because otherwise I might have written you off as a down-on-his-luck cowboy who'd stolen himself a fancy pair of boots."

"Well, Miss—" He paused, questioning her marital status.

When she nodded, he gave her a smile of approval, obviously satisfied with her answer. Different circumstances, a different time . . . and that smile might have been the one to turn her inside out. But, as usual, the circumstances were bad and the timing rotten. Not to mention the fact that the man's smile didn't quite make it to his eyes.

"Well, Miss Daniels," he continued, "you should never believe what you see. For instance, Iris doesn't look a thing like you, but you're still related."

"Well, there you go," she confessed. "I'm not

really her aunt. Just a close friend of the family. Phil's not in any trouble is he? Nothing's happened?"

"He hasn't done anything illegal, but I would like to talk to him all the same."

Behind them Iris and the butler struggled in with the bags and deposited them in the foyer with relieved sighs. Iris was the most vocal, collapsing on a specially designed metal sample case. "Jeez, Aunt Jessica, you sure don't travel light. How long are you planning on staying?"

Jessica wanted to strangle Iris for bringing up a time frame. Instead she shot the girl a warning look and said, "Only until your dad gets back, sweetie."

"When will that be?" the detective asked.

Just as soon as I find him.

Since Kincaid wouldn't appreciate the truth, she hedged, "He didn't say when he'd be back, but I'm sure he'll be checking in. Now that I'm here, if you'd like to leave a message, I could give it to him."

Those incredible eyes of his called her a liar. Then he flicked a pointed glance at the girl. "Could I speak with you privately?"

"Oh, no!" Iris said anxiously as she jumped up and came to Jessica's side. Somehow the girl's hand wound up in hers. "Is something really wrong?"

Startled by the unsolicited gesture of trust, Jessica wasn't certain what to do. Iris's palm was warm and a little damp. It felt so right and so odd nestled inside her larger hand, like she was the last line of defense between this kid and the big bad world. Right now, the big bad world had narrowed to a tall, suspicious detective with a killer smile and an agenda to go with it.

"No. There isn't anything wrong," Jessica said, meeting Kincaid's gaze and daring him to say differently.

He didn't. Not with words, but his eyes said plenty before he turned to Iris. "I need to get a few answers from your dad, and I thought he might have mentioned the information to your aunt. So I want to talk to her."

"Oh."

"Iris, why don't you go to your room? I'll take care of this." Jessica pushed her back toward the bags, wondering what a real aunt would tell her to do. Didn't mothers and caretakers constantly remind kids to do things? Finally, she called out, "Finish your homework."

Three sets of eyes swiveled toward her. The butler was smug, Kincaid curious, and Iris appalled. Not good, thought Jessica as she tried to figure out her mistake.

Iris put her out of her misery. "Homework? I don't think so. It's *June*."

"Oh. *Oh*. Summer!" Jessica nodded, the light dawning. "But don't you have summer reading or something?"

"I've done it." When Jessica opened her mouth to try again, Iris gently shook her head and started for the stairs in the hallway. "Done the reports, and Rosa helped me clean my room this morning before her mother got sick. But I'll leave anyway so you can talk about stuff you don't want me to hear." With that parting shot Iris disappeared upstairs.

Jessica took a second to regroup as Kincaid continued to stare patiently at her. He didn't undress her with his eyes, which most men seemed to get around to eventually—usually sooner rather than later. No, he did something far worse. Something that set off all her alarms. It was as if he was deciding how to take her apart psychologically. The beginning of a tingle crept up her spine.

Suddenly she didn't want to be alone with him or be the recipient of his undivided attention. There were too many questions she couldn't or didn't want to answer. There was too much unsettling energy between them. So Jessica snagged the butler's arm as he turned to leave the room.

"I'm sure you'll want to ask—" She stumbled as she realized she had no idea what the butler's name was. "—both of us some questions."

"Now that's what I like—a woman who knows what I want." Kincaid gestured them both toward the sofa and took a chair.

Jessica noticed the way he planted his feet wide and leaned toward them, his elbows resting on his thighs, hands clasped between his knees. The dark, dangerous man was gone, replaced with a good ol' boy doing his job and taking them into his confidence. Jessica wasn't fooled. No matter how drastically he altered his expression, his posture, and his voice, he couldn't mask those eyes, the restlessness that wanted an excuse to strike.

"Miss Daniels, I waited to say anything until you got here because I didn't want to upset the girl," Kincaid told them, "but yesterday we got a tip suggesting Munro might be in some danger. It's very likely a crank call. . . ."

Like hell, Jessica snapped silently. Her mind raced with possibilities as Kincaid let the silence spin out, subtly encouraging them to fill the quiet with speculation and unguarded words. Neither she nor the butler fell into the trap, and her opinion of Phil's employee went up a notch. Maybe that sprinkling of gray in his hair had been earned the old-fashioned way—through experience. Or maybe he was more than a butler.

Finally Kincaid continued, "All I want to do is verify Munro's whereabouts and inform him of our concerns. Standard procedure really."

Very slick presentation, Jessica thought. Except for the eyes; always the eyes. They cut too sharply into the people around him, soaked in every detail as he looked for anything and everything. Kincaid was beyond suspicious, she realized unhappily; he was working on a hunch. She could feel it.

Jessica swore silently. She'd have to be very careful or she'd have the police involved before she was ready. First she had to find that damn book and burn the file. Then the cops could crawl around to their hearts' content.

Trying to look unconcerned, she said, "Like you said, it was probably a crank call. Phil seemed perfectly fine when I talked to him."

"When was that exactly?"

"This morning, maybe nine o'clock. He told me something unexpected had come up. He felt bad because he'd promised to spend some time with Iris at the beach house this week and asked me to fill in. I said sure, hopped a plane to Houston and rented a car."

"And you're an old friend of the family, right?"

"Yes."

"Yet you got lost on the way to their house?"

The pregnant pause between question and answer might not have been so bad except for the unfortunately loud chime as the clock struck the half hour. Recovering, Jessica laughed and gave Kincaid a rueful grin. "I get lost on the way to the bathroom, Detective. It's a little embarrassing."

"I see."

Jessica gritted her teeth. The man had so many ways to call a person a liar without saying a word. The fact that she *was* lying didn't make it any easier to take.

Kincaid's attention never wavered from her, but his question was clearly for the butler. "When was the last time you talked to Phil Munro?"

"Not for a couple of days. But it's not unusual for Phil to travel unannounced."

Kincaid's eyes narrowed slightly as the man referred to his employer by first name. "Did Munro mention where he was going?"

"No. But then he never does."

"Phil's in the personal security business," Jessica added, aware that making Phil's huge security company sound like a bodyguard service was misleading. But it suited her purposes at the moment. "His clients are very private people. He never talks about them. It might endanger them, you see."

Sully sat back and tried to figure out what bothered him most about Miss Jessica Daniels—the glibness of her answers or the total lack of curiosity about the warning. Neither she nor Lincoln, the butler, had asked what kind of danger Phil might be in. Or if Iris was in danger. They weren't even interested in learning the name of the person who called in the tip.

Nonchalant behavior always struck him as strange. Most people were armchair detectives, insatiably curious, always ready with a theory and a laundry list of clues. So, either there was no mystery in Phil's disappearance, or these two already knew the butler did it—so to speak.

While they both waited patiently for his next question, Kincaid studied the other man. Lincoln was obviously bored, his eyes flat, and he was sitting on the edge of the cushion ready to leave. In contrast Jessica had settled in. Her dark eyes were unreadable, not a flicker of fear or surprise, but he had her complete attention.

Which meant that she had his.

The lady pushed all of his buttons—personally and professionally. She was so still—a human statue, with one arm draped along the backs of the cushions and the other across her lap. Sully got the impression she was almost daring him to focus on her instead of the situation, to rattle her. Well, he would, but not until he was damn good and ready.

When it was time to shake, rattle, and roll Jessica Daniels, there wouldn't be an audience. And there wouldn't be a coffee table between them. There wouldn't even be air between them.

"Folks, I gotta tell you," he mused. "It seems a little odd for a man to go off and leave his daughter with no way to reach him. What if she were ill?"

Lincoln shrugged. "The kid's never sick. Besides the housekeeper has a limited guardianship of Iris. Rosa's mother is ill, otherwise she'd be here twenty-four hours a day. Phil trusts her to make emergency decisions."

"How long have you been with Munro?"

"Five years with the company, four months at the house. Now, unless you've got more questions, I really need to do a perimeter check. That's what Phil pays me for—to answer the door, chauffeur the kid around, and keep an eye on the place."

Sully nodded permission as Lincoln stood up to leave. They could sit here all night and toss questions around, but it wasn't going to help. Reasonable answers didn't overrule gut instinct. His aura might be dark, but his hunches were usually red-hot. Right now he felt heat radiating from beneath the surface of Jessica's calm facade. She was hiding something.

Pulling a card out of his wallet, Sully handed it to Jessica. "I'd appreciate a call from Mr. Munro. Could you pass that message along if—"

"When," she corrected as she reached for the card. "*When* I talk to him. It'd be my pleasure, Detective Kincaid."

He held on to the card for a half beat, forcing her to look up at him before he let go. "Call me Sully. We don't stand on ceremony here on the island."

"Detective," she said, emphasizing his title. "I took one look at you and figured that out for myself." She examined his card again, and slipped it into her pocket as she walked him to the door. "We do appreciate your coming out to check on a crank call, but if there's nothing else, I'm really tired and I'd like to unpack."

Sully stopped beside the hall table and eyed her luggage. "That could take a while."

"Not really." Jessica opened the door and smiled. "I packed light this trip."

"Is that a fact?" The first real grin of the night hovered at the corners of his mouth. He could easily develop a real appreciation for the lady.

"I never lie, Detective."

"Is that a fact?" he asked softly.

"Practically a fact."

"I'll take that as a warning." He realized that their voices had dropped, and he was beginning to lean forward. Slowly he backed off. "Say good night to Iris for me."

"Say it yourself. She's been listening from the upstairs railing."

Sully swung around and caught her still on her knees. As she steadied herself, Iris gave him a look that was clearly an attempt at penance and charm. It worked.

"Don't worry," he said. "Everything's going to be fine."

The grin faded to a troubled frown. "Yes, sir."

"Good night, Iris."

"Good night."

With a last nod at Jessica, Sully started out the door only to stop cold as the significance of a small silk-wrapped rectangle on the cluttered hall table registered. He'd seen the little bundles tied with ribbon too many times that day to be mistaken. That was a deck of tarot cards. Wrapping them in silk was a ritual to keep the deck protected from unwanted psychic energies. He knew; he had asked.

Sully hated coincidences.

"Wait a minute."

He caught the door to keep it from closing and retraced his steps to the table. Beside the deck was a display of family photos, including one of Iris in a silver frame. An engraved plate below the photograph spelled out her name in ornate letters.

Iris Evangeline Munro.

The moment Sully's hand had caught the door, Jessica's thanks-for-stopping-by smile melted. She had been so close to getting rid of him! *What the hell set him off?* She shot a glance at Iris, who slowly came to her feet, staring at the detective with apprehension if not outright fear.

Not a good sign. Not a good sign at all.

Warily Jessica focused her attention on Sully. The cop stared at the table with an intensity that signaled discovery. With another glance at Iris, she suddenly realized that two people in the room knew something important, and she wasn't one of them. Her gaze raked the table, but she found only a jumble of mail, a little package, and a group of family photos. It was a portrait of Iris that had completely captured Sully's interest.

"Is there a problem, Detective?"

"Sully." He corrected her without turning. Finally he lifted the heavy silver frame. "Oh, yeah. I think there's a problem."

"And that would be?"

He handed her the frame as he swung around. "Iris Evangeline Munro."

"How clever," Jessica quipped when she noticed the name plate. "You can read."

"Between the lines and everything." Then he shot a glance up at the landing.

Jessica followed his gaze, not at all surprised to find that Iris had slipped away. The expression of dread on her face had been unmistakable. The kid hadn't wasted any time getting out of the line of fire.

"Look," Jessica said calmly, "it's been a long day, and I'm having a little trouble keeping up. So why don't you tell me what you're getting at?"

"It's real simple. We've been had by a four-foot-nothing preteen." He gave her a speculative look. Those blue eyes were incredibly direct, almost issuing a challenge. Once again she was certain the man didn't like her or that he blamed her for something. Then he raised an eyebrow. "Or at least I've been had. Maybe you knew all along."

Her brows drew together. "Just what are you implying?"

Sully ran a hand through his dark hair, tugging slightly when he got to the back of his neck. "I'm not implying anything. I'm *telling* you that I've been made a fool of. I've been chasing my tail all day, trying to locate the individual who called in the tip. The desk sergeant said the person was *ab-so-lutely* certain Munro was going to be kidnapped. But then . . . a psychic has to be pretty certain to call the police."

"Psychic?" Jessica laughed to cover the frisson of fear that swept through her when he had mentioned kidnapping. Since Iris's phone call, she'd thought of Phil as being the victim of random violence—mugged and in a hospital maybe, but not kidnapped. The coldness was brief, but it left her hands shaky.

If Phil had been kidnapped, it was for what he had. Not for the *big* bank account, but for a *little* black book. Too many people would sell their souls to control that book, and by extension the team of freelance professionals who did whatever dirty deed the government wanted done. No questions asked.

She let her laugh die away as she walked casually to the table and put the picture down. Keeping her back to him, she pretended to rearrange the frames and asked, "You've been worried about Phil because of a crackpot psychic?"

"Oh yes, ma'am," he drawled. "The thought of Mr. Munro being kidnapped gave my chief nightmares. Besides there's not much else on Jericho to keep us busy."

While she'd been fiddling with the frame, he'd stepped up behind her. So quietly that she started when he spoke. So closely that she wondered if she'd lost her instincts. Two years ago no one could have stolen up behind her, and certainly not in cowboy boots. His presence enveloped her, curling around her like night fog. Making her uncomfortably aware that she held her breath as if refusing to learn his scent would keep her safe.

Sully lowered his voice. "Phil Munro has a lot of money and a lot of power. That personal security business of his is more like an empire, isn't it?"

"Yes." Tensing, she swallowed. "But what does any of this have to do with Iris?"

"Iris *Evangeline* Munro," he repeated softly, the words humming against her ear as he leaned closer. Then he reached past her to pluck the cloth-wrapped package from the table. "Until now, I wasn't sure Madame Evangeline existed."

Instantly the significance of the name blazed through her as she stared at Iris's picture. She shook her head in denial and whirled around. Confronting him was a mistake. Sully hadn't moved more than a few inches away so she was caught between the table and his body with very little room to maneuver.

Caught. That's how she felt. Neatly snared, and for the first time in her life—out of her league.

The intimacy didn't seem to affect Sully at all, but Jessica had trouble breathing normally. Men hadn't been a part of her life for so long, she'd forgotten what it felt like to be so close or to have to look up when she spoke. Sully was one of those men who filled a room even from a distance. This close her rusty hormones couldn't tell the difference between the adrenaline of danger and the excitement of arousal. Her reaction to Sullivan Kincaid might tempt her to something stupid if she wasn't very careful.

She slowed her pulse as she lifted her gaze to his, struck all over again by the intensity he could project. More calmly than she thought possible, she said, "Tell me you aren't suggesting what I think you're suggesting about Iris."

"She looks so innocent, doesn't she?" Sully finally stepped back. He untied the ribbon and peeled back the silk to show her a deck of cards. "This is a deck of tarot cards—like psychics and fortune-tellers use. The only slip little Goldilocks made was the question 'Is something *really* wrong?'" He shook his head. "I missed that the first time. But now I think I'm going to need to talk to Madame Evangeline."

"Take a number," Jessica told him sharply, not certain whether to strangle Iris for calling the police or jump for joy that the kidnapping threat was unfounded. She walked to the bottom of the stairs, glad for the excuse to move away from Sully. "Iris, get down here."

She didn't bother to raise her voice. The kid was still eavesdropping. She'd bet on it. When the blond head poked out of the hallway to the left of the landing, Jessica crooked her finger.

Slowly Iris inched out onto the landing. The big military boots were gone, and she was barefoot. Fleetingly Jessica wondered if Iris intentionally reinforced the image of a defenseless child. Probably, and it worked because she was swamped with the sudden need to protect Iris from all the unpleasantness, all the bad things in the world.

Jessica sighed and put her hands on her hips. She was really going to have to get over this maternal thing or Iris would be leading her around by the nose. Turning to Sully, who had come to stand beside her, she found he wasn't watching Iris. He was watching her. Something in those suspicious cop eyes of his had subtly changed.

No, not changed. Something had been added. Humor. He was laughing at her.

"This is not funny," she whispered.

"No, it isn't." The humor winked out and regret replaced it. Very softly he said, "I'm going to have to take her downtown and explain exactly how serious prank calls are."

Jessica's stomach flipped. The last thing she needed was to have Iris taken down to the police station as some sort of "lesson" for wayward juveniles. She motioned for Iris to come down and wait at the foot of the stairs. Then she dragged Sully into the living room.

Out of earshot she whispered, "You can't be serious about taking her to the station for a prank! We don't even know she did it yet."

"That's what we were fixing to find out before you mauled me. Not that I'm complainin', you understand, but the tie's silk."

Jessica had one hand locked around his impressive biceps and the other had a death grip on his expensive Looney Tune tie. She was making one mistake after another with this man. Her only excuse was that she was used to having a great deal more information in situations than the skimpy bits and pieces she had at the moment.

Taking a deep breath, she let go and carefully smoothed the Tasmanian devil tie. A hard washboard of muscles rose and fell beneath her fingers as she reached the tip of his tie. Heat flamed her cheeks as she suddenly realized she'd taken an inordinately long time to perform the simple task. Sully seemed perfectly content to let her make a fool of herself.

She pulled away and flashed a contrite smile. "Sorry, I get carried away sometimes."

"No apology necessary. And just for future reference—" His voice was low, and yet it resonated inside her. "—I don't consider that a fault."

Jessica sucked in a breath as she realized Sully wasn't referring to women who got carried away in public. *Oh, God.* She really was out of practice at this.

Or Sully wasn't the kind of man who could be managed. Swallowing, she forced the subject back to safer territory. "Look, Iris is just a little girl. I want to talk to her first. Alone."

"Of course, but we can both add two and two. We know the kid did it. You've got three minutes, but then it's my turn."

"Of course," she echoed his easy agreement.

By then the lie will be ironed out.

Iris waited for her at the foot of the stairs. She had her father's serious frown, but the familiar facial expression didn't disturb Jessica nearly as much as the penetrating gaze. Involuntarily she took a step backward as recognition flooded her. Her sister, Jenny, had looked at people like that, like she could see what was written on their souls.

Uneasy, Jessica wondered what Iris could see. None of it pretty; in her case beauty was truly no more than skin deep. She was bad to the bone, born that way. Always the bad twin, the one who started all of the trouble, the one who survived.

The one with blood on her hands.

"Don't look at me like that." The words were colder than she intended, and Iris lowered her gaze to the floor.

Great. Jessica sighed again.

Obviously she was going to make mistakes with Iris too. Why the hell had she let herself get talked into this mess? Because she had no choice. With Phil missing, the past threatened her present. But those reasons were only the public truth. Jessica knew exactly why she was here.

Because she wanted to be the good guy for once.

Iris had no idea what Jessica really was. The girl thought she was one of her father's elite bodyguards, one of the chosen few her dad respected. One of the few her dad trusted. Iris had faith in her, and that was the scariest part of the job. Faith was so fragile; she knew. Maybe this time it would be different.

She looked over her shoulder to make certain that Sully had kept his word about waiting in the living room. "Iris, did you call the police? Did you tell them you were Madame Evangeline?"

Iris didn't look up. "Yes, ma'am."

"Why? I told you *not* to call them, that I'd take care of everything, including calling the police when it was time."

Finally the girl looked up, scared but honest enough to confess when cornered. "I'd already talked to them by the time I called you."

"So why call me?"

"Because the police didn't feel right."

"Didn't feel right?" Jessica echoed, bewildered.

"I can't explain it." Iris's expression pleaded with her to understand. "It was just wrong, so I hung up and called you."

Jessica huffed out a long breath and dragged her hair behind her shoulders. "So why didn't you tell me you called the police first?"

"I didn't call them first."

Needles of fear pricked the back of Jessica's neck as she imagined Iris making phone call after phone call until she found someone who felt just right. Careful to keep the apprehension out of her voice, Jessica asked, "Who did you call first?"

THREE

While Sully waited he let the piece of silk drop to the coffee table and examined the tarot deck that was still in his hand. The cards were oversize, and the back design was a yellow and brown canvas with a disturbing and very realistic eye—as if someone was looking out of the cards at him. The pictorial sides of the cards were dark, muted paintings. Many of the cards depicted people or ideas such as Justice or Temperance. Each time he looked at the pictures he saw something new, objects hidden in the background of the paintings like owls or peacock feathers or rippling water. Hell if he knew what any of it meant, though.

Sully shuffled the cards absently until Jessica and Iris came into the room. His qualms about the case, which had subsided, came roaring back as he looked at their faces. He expected Iris to be a little scared considering her prank; he expected Jessica to look embarrassed or even angry with the girl. But neither of them should have been frightened to the point of becoming pale and solemn.

What the hell had gone on out in the hall?

When Iris's eyes widened at the sight of him shuffling the deck, he stopped and held it out to her. "Awfully big cards for such small hands. Are they yours?"

"They were my mother's." Iris took them and clutched them to her chest protectively. As she spoke Sully noticed the mood ring on her index finger go black. "She died a long time ago, so I guess they're mine now."

Sometimes Sully hated his job. Right now was one of those times. "Sit down, Iris."

Jessica gave Iris a reassuring squeeze on the shoulder and stood beside her as the girl took a seat in one of the striped chairs. With her back ramrod straight Iris looked very much like a condemned woman waiting for last rites. Sully looked up, his gaze marking Jessica. Slowly her head came up, her eyes soft and gentle for a moment before she shifted gears to mother tigress. Seconds passed before Sully realized he hadn't begun. Clearing his throat and crossing his arms, he asked the obvious question.

"Did you call the police last night? Tell us you were Madame Evangeline and that your father was going to be kidnapped?"

Her eyes dropped. "Yes, sir."

"Did you have a reason to be worried about your father?"

Iris looked up at Jessica, but he couldn't tell if it was for support or coaching. "No."

"Why did you call, Iris?" he pressed, moving to hunker down beside her so she had to look at him and not Jessica. "Were you mad at your dad? Did you do this for attention?"

"Of course not! I'm not a baby!" Some of the attitude was back, and that made him feel less the bad guy. She rubbed her fingers across the cards. "I get these feelings sometimes. Momma had them too. Everyone says we're alike that way. Yesterday I had one of those feelings."

"Let me get this straight," Sully said trying to control his exasperation. "You called the police because of a feeling?"

Jessica spoke up for the first time, her eyes sending the message to back off. "Yes, a *feeling*, Sully. It's a seven-letter word for hunch. You know what one of those is, don't you?"

"Yeah." Sully shifted his full attention upward. He had no intention of backing off. "Isn't that when I think someone is lying to me and I can't prove it?"

Misunderstanding the byplay between the adults, Iris objected, "But I'm not lying! It *was* one of my feelings. I did a reading with the cards to see what it was about, but it didn't help this time. Lincoln and Rosa wouldn't listen. Well, Lincoln listened, and then he laughed. Rosa crossed herself like she does every time I get one of my premonitions. That's when I decided I had to do something myself before anything bad happened to my dad."

Those purple eyes of hers were suspiciously shiny. Sully wondered if Phil Munro was worthy of her tears. God knew his own father had never been worthy of a passing thought much less real concern. Iris's concern worried him, nagged at him.

"Iris, did you overhear something that scared you? Maybe someone threatening your dad? An upsetting phone call?"

She looked up at Jessica again and then said, "No, sir."

"Iris, look at me, not Miss Daniels," he ordered sharply. "Are you sure?"

"Yes, sir. It was just a feeling."

Sully wasn't satisfied, but he let the issue drop for the moment. "Why didn't you tell the police who you really were?"

"I got scared that I was doing the wrong thing. Or that Daddy would be mad. And the policeman's voice was . . . yuck. Just full of negative energy. I told him I was Madame Evangeline and hung up as quick as I could."

Negative energy? he echoed silently. She had actually shivered when she said it. Despite the number of times she had looked to Jessica for reassurance, this was not a rehearsed act. Little Iris was a bona fide New Age flake in training. Sully stood up and paced a few steps, wondering why he was surprised the day was ending exactly as it had begun—in the company of flakes.

Unfortunately, he had that tickle at the back of his neck again—the one that signaled trouble. Something wasn't right, but he couldn't get a handle on it. Maybe his instincts just needed more time to adjust to a life away from the *badlands* and bad guys. He was so used to being lied to that he assumed the worst. Even of children.

"Mr. Kincaid, I didn't mean to make trouble."

"She didn't," Jessica instantly seconded. "Can't we just forget this ever happened?"

At her question he stopped pacing. It was tempting, if for no other reason than he could walk away and the lady would owe him one. Turning to face them, he was struck by the contrasts between the two. Jessica was as dark as Iris was fair. One was an abundantly sexy woman; the other was barely past skinned knees and teddy bears. Most disturbing of all was his impression that the aunt was as guilty as the girl was innocent.

Iris was certainly a far cry from his usual brand of bad guy. She was shorter, younger, and unarmed. But no matter how sincere her actions might have been, what she did was wrong. He had to impress upon her the seriousness of involving the police without facts. It was his *job* to cut short the career of Madame Evangeline and put the fear of God in Iris.

So, why did he feel like an ogre? Because only monsters frightened children. Sully knew all about monsters. He'd lived with one for sixteen years and hunted them for almost as long. And then there was the nagging feeling that more was going on here than met the eye.

Finally making a decision, he spoke to Jessica, "Iris made a false report to the police. This isn't something we normally ignore."

Jessica straightened as she realized what he was trying to convey without tipping Iris. She had barely mouthed a relieved thank-you before he focused on the girl.

As Jessica watched him, she wondered if he knew how uncomfortable he looked. Obviously reading the riot act to children wasn't standard procedure for him. Jessica imagined taking a bullet was higher on the list of things he'd rather be doing.

"Iris, do you know what it means to cry wolf?" he asked sharply.

"Yes, sir."

"Good. Because crying wolf is what you did with that stunt of yours. I've wasted an entire day questioning people who had better things to do than talk to me about a hoax."

"I-I'm sorry."

"Next time you call the police, we might not believe you."

"I didn't think about that."

"Well, you think about it, and while you're thinking, think about the money you cost this city. Money that your daddy may be asked to pay."

"Couldn't I pay you back out of my allowance instead? I don't mind. I have a lot saved up."

Sully looked nonplussed for a moment, like he'd had all the air knocked out of him. Jessica knew just how he felt. Iris had managed to knock the wind out of her sails a few times. She was an unusual child, an odd blend of naïveté and wisdom. She had a way of looking at a person that cut right to the soul. So did Sully, but he did more than look at her. He talked to her; he touched her; he got to her.

Taking a minute to recover from Iris's earnest offer of repayment, Sully crossed his arms before he said, "Even if you do repay the city from your allowance, your father's going to have to be told. This is a serious matter."

"Yes, sir, I understand," Iris said, and slumped in her chair.

"Instead of taking you downtown, I'm going to leave you in the custody of Miss Daniels." When Iris sighed in relief and smiled, he added, "Next time you go to court."

The grin faded. "Yes, sir."

"And you're grounded," Jessica added firmly, hoping it was the right reaction to Sully's lecture. He didn't seem impressed.

"You." He pointed at her and inclined his head toward the foyer. "I've got a few more things to say."

"Of course you do," she mumbled quietly as she followed him.

Looking behind her, Jessica saw Iris slip out of the chair and begin laying out cards on the coffee table.

Before she could ask what it was all about, Sully took her arm and marshaled her past her luggage and out the door into the hot summer night.

Although a breeze came off the ocean, it did little more than push the heat around. Not that Sully needed any help pushing heat or her around at the moment. He was the cop, and obviously used to being in control.

He didn't stop until they'd walked a few paces to the edge of the gently curved drive, which looped around the front yard of the estate and back to the gate. When he let go of her arm, he seemed to do it in slow motion. Like the earlier handshake, his touch lingered a second longer than necessary. The pads of his fingers left warm spots behind.

"Fair warning, Jessie. I'm going to be keeping my eye on the two of you."

"My name is Jessica," she told him, barely resisting the urge to rub her arm where his fingers had rested. "And not to seem ungrateful for the attention of a big, strong man, but what on earth for? There's nothing wrong. I grounded her. Case closed."

"Call it a hunch. You know, a five-letter word for feeling."

"Oh, come on, Sully," she cajoled, unable to keep the edge out of her voice and horrified that he wanted to keep digging. "This is nothing but a little girl's overactive imagination!"

"Then you shouldn't mind my dropping in from time to time until I'm satisfied on that point."

"Well, that depends on how often you'll be droppin' in," she snapped and began to pull her windblown hair away from her face. "I'm afraid it might be a lot since you don't strike me as a man who's easily satisfied. Ow!"

A strand of hair had gotten caught in the clasp of her watch. She sucked in another sharp breath and halted, arm half-lowered, not wanting to rip out any more hair and feeling incredibly stupid. Without waiting for an invitation, Sully reached to untangle the strand and then tucked it behind her ear. His fingers trailed gently around the shell of her ear, and once again she felt trapped in the odd never-never land of sensation that his touch created. The contact was too brief to be sensual and yet lasted too long to be ignored. Anticipation swirled through her, only to die as he dropped his hand away.

"I'm not easily satisfied, but not to worry, Jessica. You haven't got anything to hide, have you?"

Plenty, Jessica thought. The prospect of trying to hide it from Sully made her uneasy. As usual he stood too close. Or maybe the night was too small to swallow him up the way it would have a lesser man. By design or happenstance, he'd picked one of the few spots not completely illuminated by floodlights. Jessica didn't think Sullivan Kincaid did much of anything by accident. He struck her as the deliberate type.

Holding her arms out from her sides and in her best Texas belle drawl, she tried to deflect the question with teasing. "Now what would I have to hide?"

"Darlin', everybody's got something to hide."

"Except you, of course," she noted sourly, letting her hands fall to her hips.

"No, I imagine I have more to hide than most."

Sully wanted the words back as soon as they left his mouth. He hadn't meant to be honest, and certainly not with this woman, one he hardly knew and suspected of . . . something. The lighting was too uncertain to trust the surprising flicker of understanding in her eyes at his confession. Then the cool, familiar mask descended, and she laughed.

"Do women actually fall for that line?"

"Line?"

"When you pretend to be the dark, wounded man who suffers in private torment while looking for a soul mate who can understand him?"

"Oh that line. Yeah, it works most of the time," he lied. In point of fact, Sully didn't know whether it worked or not. He'd never tried it. "And for future reference, just what kind of line would you have fallen for?"

"Oh, I don't fall." Her answer was quick, her tone final.

"Then I guess my only hope is to trip you up."

At his throwaway quip, he thought he saw fear steal into her expression, and that pulse of suspicion began to throb in his gut again. The lady was scared of him. The only question was why? What was she hiding?

She recovered quickly, pursing her lips as she considered him. She toyed with the neckline of her silk shirt and finally met his gaze. She could have given the night lessons on sultry.

"Trip me up? You can try, but the only thing you're going to put to bed around here is this ridiculous *case*. So you drop by anytime you feel like it, Sully. I look forward to seeing you fail."

He wasn't fooled by her sudden willingness to play sexpot; she obviously intended to offer herself as a challenge to take his mind off of Phil Munro. To make the game interesting he gave her some advice. "Instead of looking forward, you better be looking behind you. I don't generally play by the rules."

"What a coincidence. Neither do I. Good night, Detective."

"Aww . . . we're suddenly back to 'detective.' How'd that happen? We were doing so well."

"My good sense returned," she explained as she walked away.

He couldn't help but laugh. "Good night, *Miss Daniels.* You have Munro call me."

"As soon as I hear from him."

"The sooner the better," he yelled at her retreating back.

She slipped in the door without a backward glance. Left in the dark Sully realized the sway of that woman's walk was going to haunt his thoughts for the better part of the night. Just as she intended. She was dark and mysterious—an enigma. No, a chameleon would be a better description—cool one minute, shy the next, and a flirt challenging him the moment after that. With no rhyme or reason to explain the transitions.

Inconsistency intrigued him as much as coincidence irritated him. And, at the moment, she was the *only* intriguing game on an island that thrived on peace and quiet and dull routine.

Sully shook his head and started the long walk down the drive to his car. He stopped only long enough to look through the window of her rental car. As he hoped, her customer info packet had been tossed carelessly on the dashboard.

Checking to make sure no one watched, Sully leaned over the windshield until he could read the upside-down company name printed in bold logo-type letters on the folder. Good. A nice national company with rules and lots of forms filled out in triplicate.

The rental agency ought to have enough information to point him in the right direction. He'd have one of his old buddies in Houston pay them a visit first thing in the morning. By tomorrow afternoon he'd have a head start on tripping up Miss Daniels. He tugged his tie loose and headed for his car.

A tiny internal voice, one he rarely listened to, warned him that Jessica stirred something inside him that was better left untouched, unexplored. The other voice, the one he always listened to, told him it was too late to worry about that now.

The game was afoot.

As rapidly as she could, Iris laid out a spread from the cards shuffled by the detective. The man hadn't agreed to be the subject of a reading. He probably didn't center and focus before he shuffled, which could mean a reading that was psychically all over the place. But a muddled reading was better than no reading at all.

Especially now that she had the feeling she needed both Jessica and Kincaid to find her dad. When they were in a room together, it was like one flow of energy instead of two. They were connected somehow. She knew that much; she could feel it.

Iris's eyes widened as the cards fell. When the last one was placed, she set the deck aside and began to study them—looking for patterns and the flow of his story. Exhaling slowly, Iris realized Jessica wasn't going to like this at all.

She was already angry about the phone calls. Of course Iris figured that Jessica would get over being angry, so it didn't bother her too much. The sadness in her eyes and soul did bother her; that wouldn't go away so easily. When she'd slipped her hand into Jessica's, emptiness and regret had come through loud and clear. It almost felt like Jessica wasn't whole.

Iris wrapped her fingers around the harmony ball that hung on a heavy silver chain from her neck. The motion caused the faint chiming sounds that always gave her comfort. Briefly she wondered if she should give the necklace to Jessica.

At that moment, the door opened and closed with a whoosh of negative energy. Maybe not, Iris decided. She needed it herself right now.

After Jessica'd had enough time to walk the distance from the foyer to the coffee table, Iris announced, "We got ourselves a problem."

"We've got ourselves a problem?" the woman echoed as she came to stand beside her. "*A* problem, Iris? Try four problems. One: According to you, your father's fallen off the face of the earth because he didn't make his scheduled never-miss Sunday phone call to you. Two: I've got a suspicious detective on my hands because you called the police."

Jessica sat down and rested her elbows on her knees and her head in her hands for a second. "Sully was right about you. You are Goldilocks, which brings us to problem number three: I can't believe you called the CIA before you called the police!"

"I already explained that. I didn't know they felt cold until I talked to them."

"Of course not. It all makes perfect sense. The CIA was cold. The police were full of negative energy, and lucky me—I was 'just right.' "

"You were. As soon as I heard your voice, I knew you were the only one who could find Daddy."

"Well, that's problem number four: I've got maybe forty-eight hours to find your dad before the police figure out he's really missing and come after Madame Evangeline and Jessica Daniels as their prime suspects."

Frowning, Iris shook her head and lifted her eyes from the tarot cards. "Um . . . I don't think you have that long. He's after you already."

"That much is obvious. The man probably chases everything in a skirt." She pulled on the cuffs of her khakis. "Or in shorts."

"I don't mean like that." Iris took a deep breath and got it over with. "He's hunting you. It's like he's following a trail."

"Where would you get an idea like that?"

Iris pointed at the spread in front of her. "He handled the cards. I did a reading on him."

"Oh, great. Maybe we can get out the Ouija board and find your dad." Jessica sighed, realizing how short she sounded, and leaned forward. The section of hair with the white streak brushed the coffee table as she did. "Iris, I don't believe in tarot cards or crystal balls. All that stuff we said about your *feelings* and the cards was just to fool Sully. To get rid of him."

"You're in the reading." Iris knew that would get her attention. People loved to hear about themselves.

"Me?"

Iris picked a card up and handed it to her. "The Empress."

Hesitantly Jessica took the card and looked down at it, surprised by its sensual nature. The card's predominant figure was a naked woman standing in a moonlike boat with a snake twined around one arm and some kind of staff in the other hand. "Does your dad know you have these cards?"

"Of course he does! There isn't anything here I haven't seen in sex education. I *am* twelve."

"Right. Twelve. Naked snake ladies in sixth grade. Where have I been?" She handed the card back. "So should I be insulted or impressed with myself?"

"Scared. Major Arcana cards mean it's out of your control. I don't think you can stop whatever's going to happen between you and the detective."

Smiling, Jessica said, "Believe me. I am in complete control."

"Not a chance." Iris tucked her hair behind her ear and began pointing out cards. "Here. This card, where it all begins. It's *so* strong; this part is so cool. He's a hunter who seeks prey to escape his own darkness. And it's capped by the Wheel of Fortune, which means something has changed, been set in motion by cosmic forces. Which is probably the problem with my dad. See the hand reaching up to grab hold of the wheel?"

Stunned by Iris's performance—Jessica didn't quite know what else to call it—she asked, "How do you know all this?"

"I read about tarot."

"You can't get all this from books."

"Sure you can. All you need is a great memory. I've got one of those. I read two thick books just about this one deck, and I've read all about symbols and colors and numerology and *I Ching*. It's all here in the cards. Once you memorize all the meanings, you just have to read the pictures and the symbols." Iris lifted her eyes to make sure Jessica was ready to go on.

Jessica nodded.

"Okay," Iris said. "Tarot is like a story. This is where the Empress comes in. That's how he sees the situation. She's the card of passion, of energy. And love. I don't mean kissy-face Valentine's Day love. I'm talking about major emotional stuff. That's represented by the water. See it rocks the boat."

Drawn into the bizarreness in spite of herself, Jessica made a connection to Sully, and she felt the tiny hairs on the back of her neck prickle. "He doesn't like the boat rocked."

"Not the way the Empress rocks it. It's too real. He doesn't like real. That's what he's afraid of." She tapped another card. "He doesn't like being human. He fears the devil in himself, but he's drawn to the Empress and she's about as real as you can get. She's good and bad."

Jessica's heart skipped a beat. "W-what?"

"Oh, I didn't mean *you* were bad. The Empress is human. That snake represents"—Iris frowned and closed her eyes as she struggled for the right word—"*transformation!* Because of how it sheds its skin. That's change, right? Some people say it also means evil, that desire and evil are a part of the Empress card just like love is."

"A part that she tries to hold away from herself," Jessica whispered.

"Cool! It does seem like she's holding the snake away. Or trying to. I never noticed that before. It doesn't work, though."

I know, Jessica agreed silently. "Iris, what does any of this have to do with your father being missing?"

"Everything in this reading points to you. The detective can't see anything but you. I don't know what you did to set him off, but he thinks you're the key. The cards are about pursuit and getting justice. He's a hunter. If he's hunting, then he's hunting you. Well, there's his father, but that's in his past—"

"Where?"

"This one. It's the only other people card in the reading. It's the Father of Cups in the North. He's like a majorly powerful father figure. A very emotional father, but the card's upside down." Iris's expression was grim. "That means something went wrong in their relationship. Bad wrong."

Jessica shivered as she remembered what Sully had said about having more to hide than most. Quiet descended on the room as Iris waited for her to ask another question. Instead Jessica told her to put the cards away. She didn't want to know anything more about Sullivan Kincaid. Or her attraction to him.

Whoa! she told herself as she realized the trap she'd fallen into. No matter how convincingly Iris spun her tale, these cards were just a game. They couldn't tell her anything about Sully. She didn't believe a word of it. Not a word.

"I need to look at your dad's calendar and his papers. Maybe I can find a lead. Where's his office or study?"

"Off the TV room, but it's always locked."

"Who's got a key?"

"Daddy."

"How about the housekeeper or Lincoln?"

"Lincoln doesn't, and Rosa's not here. She's been going home at night lately to take care of her mother."

"Okay, we'll improvise." Jessica stopped in the foyer, unzipped one of her bags, and drew out a lock-pick kit. "Lead the way."

The office was toward the back of the house, off of an entertainment room that held two large-screen TV's and a wall of videos and CD's. The airy seascape pastels in the rest of the house gave way to bold burgundies and greens. Crossing the threshold into the entertainment room was like crossing the border between peacefully coexisting countries.

Iris stopped suddenly. She put a hand on Jessica's arm and silently directed her attention to the double doors on the left side of the room. They led to the office.

One of them was ajar.

FOUR

Simultaneously Jessica swept Iris behind her and reached inside the neckline of her blouse. A custom-made stacked barrel derringer nestled between her breasts, hidden in her bra. The weapon was so small, she could almost palm it, but there was nothing small about the two hollow point bullets. Sliding the gun gently from its hiding place, she thumbed the safety off.

Surprised by how easily she'd slipped back into old habits—like carrying the derringer, Jessica assessed the room in a way that had nothing to do with decoration. The windows to the right were shut; no panes were broken, no signs of entry. The only other ways in or out of the entertainment room were through the double doors leading to Phil's office and through the hallway behind them.

She glanced over her shoulder, assuring herself that the corridor was empty. Then she eased her way around the two leather sofas toward the office door.

Iris clutched the back of Jessica's shirt with both hands and followed her like a shadow. Thankfully, Iris was smart enough to keep silent; she hadn't asked a single question. Given a choice, Jessica would have preferred to investigate alone, but she had no choice right now. If something went wrong, the kid was safer with her than standing like a target in the doorway.

Taking care to stay out of sight of anyone inside the office, Jessica worked her way to the edge of the double doors. She stopped beside the one which was still closed and listened to the ominous silence around them. Without knowing who or what waited for them behind the door, even the simple act of breathing seemed a dangerous risk to take.

Suddenly an eerie sense of déjà vu swamped Jessica. She remembered another time, another door. Every detail came rushing back with frightening clarity. She became a scared young girl again, hiding behind a door and clutching a small piece of glass. Hoping it would be enough.

Closing her eyes for the briefest second, she cleared her mind, shoving the past back where it belonged. Shoving it away before the fear could grab hold of her and pull her further into the nightmare. When her pulse settled, she handed Iris the small zippered lock kit. Then, with her foot, she gave the partially opened door a nudge, half expecting someone to lunge out of the room or send a bullet through the opening. No one did, and the door swung wide.

When the handle banged against the wall, a masculine voice startled them both. "Oh for God's sake! Stop skulking around out there and come in."

Stunned, Jessica realized it was Lincoln's voice and eased her head past the door. He stood beside the desk, gingerly holding the phone receiver with two fingers and looking expectantly in her direction. At the moment he resembled a butler more than a security guard, but she knew better than to trust impressions. Using the door to shield her actions, Jessica slipped the derringer into the pocket of her shorts and then stepped into the office. Any relief she felt was instantly erased by his next command.

"Don't touch anything. We may have been burglarized."

She froze and tried to calculate how much time it would take the CIA to get someone to Texas. Iris had stumbled on to Phil's contact by pushing the redial on his bedroom phone. So Jessica had to figure they were coming, the only question was when. They'd want that book, too, and anything else that might establish a connection between the "company" and Phil.

He'd never actually said which branch of the government gave the orders, but it had been fairly obvious from the targets. The CIA wouldn't want a trail of bread crumbs leading to their doorstep. They'd used Phil because they wanted to maintain deniability; a link to him would defeat the whole purpose of free-lance operatives.

But . . . was Phil *still* working for them? A lot could change in two years. If Phil had refused to work with them, some very bad people would be very cranky. Cranky enough to take Phil out and wipe the slate clean? She didn't know.

Where are you, Phil? And what have you done?

Not quit, she decided. He wouldn't quit. He liked the cloak-and-dagger too much. Jessica scrutinized the office around her. The vague disarray could just as easily have been caused by a rapid search for the address book as by Phil's disorganized work habits.

Afraid she already knew the answer, she asked, "What was taken?"

"I don't know. I haven't exactly checked," Lincoln

snapped. "I wouldn't know anyway since I've never been in here, but the door was unlocked. Phil's the only one with a key." He gave her a speculative glance. "Regardless of Iris's devotion to you, Miss Daniels, if you hadn't been with the detective, you'd be the first person on my short list of suspects."

Jessica returned his gaze without flinching. The man was right to be distrustful of her. She'd come here with every intention of tossing Phil's office. Somebody just beat her to it.

"But I *was* with the detective," she reminded him. "And the housekeeper's gone. That leaves only you or Iris."

"That's why I'm calling the police," he said, and bent toward the phone.

"No!" Both Iris and Jessica shouted the word with such conviction that Lincoln actually backed up a step.

"Excuse me?"

Before Jessica could explain, Iris shot forward and took the phone out of Lincoln's hand. "The police are already mad at me, Linc, because I called them about my dad."

The man sighed heavily and rolled his head in disgust. "Iris, honey, tell me you weren't the one who called them with that cock-and-bull story about your dad being in danger!"

"I wish I hadn't, Linc. Really. I'm sorry, but I did. So don't you see? We absolutely *cannot* call them again unless we're sure. Or they'll just say it was me making something up and crying wolf again. And next time the detective said I had to go to jail."

"She's right," Jessica agreed. She had her own reasons for wanting to keep the police out of it for a while longer. Especially Sully Kincaid. He was far too perceptive. He didn't need any more fuel for his hunch.

"The man was not a happy camper," she warned. "Before we do anything, we need to be certain of what happened. I assume Phil hired you because you were good. So, tell me, Lincoln, how could someone get in here without your knowing it?"

"If you'd asked me an hour ago, I would have told you it was impossible." He was as serious as a man could be. "None of the window alarms tripped. The sensors on the outside wall didn't trip. There's no sign of entry. Except an unlocked door."

"So maybe no one got in. Maybe Phil didn't pull the door all the way shut. Maybe it didn't latch and just finally popped open tonight. Have you tried it lately? Do you know for sure that it was locked?"

She could tell he wanted to believe the tidy explanation she'd wrapped up and tied with ribbon for him. He almost did, and then she lost him. The man was too much of a professional to accept absolution that easily.

Lincoln shook his head. "Phil's not careless."

"He was probably in a hurry." Safe guess, Jessica thought. Ever since she'd known Phil, he'd been in a hurry. "Take a look at the facts. You don't know if anything's missing. You don't know how someone got in. You can't even swear the door was locked. How's that going to sound to Detective Kincaid?"

"Linc, you should have heard him," Iris added. "He was really mad at me."

Jessica kept the smile of satisfaction off her face as Lincoln rubbed his eyes. The man was caving. Who wouldn't when big purple eyes begged so prettily? Iris offered to help him look around, check to see if anything was missing. Jessica helped too.

Five minutes later, she had done as thorough a job of searching the office as she could with eyewitnesses in the room. As far as she could tell, beyond income tax records, there was nothing of importance to steal. She didn't even know why Phil bothered to lock the room. *Unless there was a hidden safe they hadn't been able to find yet.* Sighing, she sat down in the chair, about to pronounce the office unmolested. Then her eyes fell on the desk calendar.

It was one of those designs with loose sheets to flip over each day. She stared at it, something nagging her. And then she noticed, this one was missing pages. About a week's worth. The last week's worth.

Sully was way out of his jurisdiction, and he knew it. He could have made a phone call this morning and had his buddies in Houston check out the rental agency. But he hadn't. Nor did he have any real business swinging by Munro Security on his way back to Jericho. But since he was already in Houston . . . and only a few miles away . . . Why not? In for a penny, in for a pound.

Never one to lie to himself, he admitted his impulsive trip to Houston was more personal reconnaissance than real investigation. Sure, vague cop alarms were going off in his head after last night, but they were drowned out by the clamoring of his libido. That hadn't happened for a long time.

Not like this. Not with a woman he hardly knew. He wanted more than hot sex, although he didn't deny a strong physical pull or the need to touch Jessica Daniels. Sure, he wanted to hear her voice in the dark, all sleepy and satisfied, but he also wanted to know about that streak of white in her hair. He wanted to get inside her head. He wanted to know why her eyes gave the impression she'd been to hell and back. Maybe more than once.

Jessica Daniels intrigued him, and that worried him. He was drawn to her by something he couldn't name, something hot and dark beneath the surface. They were mirror images—two predators on neutral territory, circling, testing, and retreating. When they got too close, heat pulsed between them. Jessica chose to ignore it, but Sully figured he'd better pay attention.

Nothing good ever came from ignoring what was slapping you in the face. He'd learned that lesson at his mother's knee while she iced her swollen jaw and kissed the lingering handprint on his cheek. All the while she told him that his father wasn't really a drunk. His father didn't *want* to beat them, she explained so softly, so sincerely. His father loved them. That's why he had to be so firm with them. He wanted only the best for them.

His mother had ignored the bad things, replacing them with fantasies and rationalizations. Ignorance wasn't bliss; it was hell. His mother had died in hell, and if divine justice existed, the violent bastard who killed her was rotting there as well.

Sully never forgot the sins of the father. He couldn't afford to; the same blood ran in his veins, the same capacity for violence. He suspected that just might be the reason his angel wept.

Another point Jessica and I have in common, Sully decided instinctively. With eyes like that surely her angel was weeping too. The only question was why? What did Jessica regret? What secrets did she hide?

He pondered the possibilities as he turned onto Westheimer. The Munro complex, two high-rise office buildings connected by a walkway, was a couple of short blocks up on the left. All he intended to do was ask Munro's secretary a few routine follow-up questions to yesterday's telephone interview. And maybe casually mention Jessica's name to gauge her response.

But what he'd planned to do was forgotten an instant later. Bright sunlight flashed and winked as it bounced off a familiar metallic-blue sedan carrying two passengers. Sully's fingers tensed around the wheel, and he increased speed as the sedan—only a block away—whipped into the Munro company parking lot. Cursing, he slowed his car for a red light and watched the sedan disappear through the gate.

What on earth were Jessica and Iris doing here?

By the time he'd made it through the stoplight and security gate, they had five minutes on him. He'd wasted enough time at the gate, he didn't want to waste time with the receptionist or alert Jessica he was on the way up. So as he approached the reception desk, he feigned shortness of breath.

"Sullivan Kincaid. Looks like I'm late again. Did Iris already go up?" He tapped the counter with his hand and zipped past toward the elevators without waiting for an answer. "Can you believe it? Lord, I told Phil I'd be here for this! Which office are they using?"

The receptionist, obviously the softhearted type, bought his harried act and sheepish grin without a second thought and waved him on. "Go! Go! I'll sign you in." They went to Mr. Munro's office. Tenth floor. She did look a little worried. "If you hurry, you can probably catch them before they notice you're late!"

Yeah, he wanted to catch them all right—red-handed. They were up to something. Why else would Jessica drag Iris up to Houston with Phil gone? This was a helluva long way to come for free pencils. The elevator barely opened before he was out. The tenth floor was obviously executive country judging from the softly lit sculptures lining the corridors.

The place was deserted at lunch. Except for Iris, who seemed to be standing guard in front of a massive mahogany door at the end of a short hallway to his left. Fortunately she was tying her shoe at the moment. When she finally looked up and saw him, her eyes widened, and her mouth dropped open.

"Don't," he advised softly with a shake of his head. "Don't say, shout, or sing a word." He halted beside the empty secretarial alcove, lowering his voice even more. "Is that your dad's office? She in there?"

Both questions were answered with quick nods. The anguished look on Iris's face and the way she kept cutting her eyes toward the door confirmed his hunch that this wasn't a casual tour of the office.

"Did your dad call and ask you to meet him? To pick up something?" When Iris shook her head, he said, "Didn't think so. You stay. I'm gonna have a private chat with your aunt Jessica."

As quietly as possible he eased the door open and then closed it behind him. Jessica's back was to him as she bent over the calendar on Munro's desk. The view of her rump wasn't bad, but he wasn't here to inventory her assets.

"Iris," she whispered as she ripped out a page. "I told you to give me ten minutes."

"You sure that'll be enough?"

Jessica jumped at the sound of his voice, crumpling the paper in her hand as she clenched her fist, but she didn't scream. She didn't utter a sound. That surprised him. Sully leaned against the door, crossed his arms, and waited for her to turn around. When she did, the woman looked as guilty as sin. And sexy as hell.

The hip-hugging denim skirt she wore was short

and sweet. Her cowboy boots had engraved toeplates, and her shirt was one of those loose, sleeveless crop tops that buttoned up the front and exposed skin every time she moved. He sure did like the way she moved. It was a shame she was so damned slippery.

"A bit jumpy are we?" he queried softly. "Why is that? It wouldn't be because we're hiding something from the police, would it?"

"I'm not *hiding* anything." She lifted her chin. The view of her neck wasn't bad either. "If you must know. . . ."

"Oh, I'm afraid I must."

"I'm checking Phil's calendar for Iris's orthodontist appointment."

"She doesn't wear braces."

"She's getting them."

He smiled. "Who's the orthodontist?"

She hesitated a second too long.

"Thought so." Sully pushed away from the door and held out his hand for the calendar page.

"Look, Sully, chill out." She casually smoothed and folded the calendar page. "I'll confess. You seemed so insistent about talking to Phil, and I thought I'd try to track him down by snooping through his schedule."

"He calls in, doesn't he? That's what you said last night. So why look for him?" Sully walked toward her as he spoke. "Why lie about orthodontists? Unless he's really missing. Is Phil Munro really missing, Jessie?"

Jessica cursed silently and retreated. She didn't have an answer for him. Not yet.

The closer he got, the faster her pulse raced. She couldn't banish the image of a predator from her mind. Not when the personification of the word stalked her in broad daylight. She was his prey. That much was obvious, and it scared the hell out of her.

The fear that sped her heart had nothing to do with safety. Not physical safety. A threat like that she could have handled. She'd killed men who had been bigger and stronger than Sully, men who deserved to die for unspeakable acts, but she wondered if any of them had been more dangerous, more intense.

The way Sully looked at her made her wonder how thin his veneer of civility was. Made her wonder what the hell a man like him was doing on Jericho Island. The stone-cold glare that accompanied his question made her think twice about lying to him. But she did anyway.

"I really don't like your tone. And I don't know how many times I'm gonna have to tell you this. Phil is fine. I came down here to look at a stupid calendar. So what? It's not a crime."

"Not unless you're destroying evidence."

Jessica backed up another step and kept backing up. She was unhappy with herself for giving way but unable to stop her feet from retreating. Every brain cell she had was scrambling to process the jumble of sensation that came with being in the same room with the man and the object of his undivided attention. The easiest way to deal with the unfamiliar feelings was to create some distance. Unfortunately he wasn't getting the message, because he just kept coming. Thank God Phil's office was huge.

"Sully, Sully, Sully . . . you've got to be kidding. Destroying *evidence*? There is no evidence! There is no crime! And while I'm on the subject, why are you here? Aren't you just a bit out of your jurisdiction? You act like you're following up on some big case instead of a little schoolgirl prank!"

"Oh, but I don't think it's a prank. I think something scared that kid. Something she's not telling. And

I imagine you know what it is. I imagine you told her not to tell."

"Cops have such active fantasy lives," she said cuttingly.

He didn't deny it; she almost wished he had. Instead he raised an eyebrow and smiled knowingly as she backed herself into a corner. Her shoulders came up against the walls.

"Darlin', you'd be surprised at what I can imagine given just a tiny bit of inspiration." His voice was low, full of innuendo.

"Appalled would probably be more like it."

He laughed. "Maybe, but my money's on . . . fascinated. Your eyes are too hungry for you to be appalled at much of anything sexual, Jessie. So take my advice—leave the innocent act to the innocents. Now, if you're through sweet-talkin' and sidetrackin' me, I would like to see that schedule."

"You got a warrant?" she snapped, irritated by his ego.

"Am I going to need one?"

Resigned, Jessica gave him the page, hoping he'd back off to look at it. Sully didn't move anywhere, effectively trapping her in the corner. Nor did he glance at the sheet in his hand, his gaze never wavering from hers.

The beginning of a shiver slid up Jessica's spine, but she resisted the urge to look away. "Hey, I gave it to you, Sully. Do you think you can stop trying to intimidate me now?"

"The only thing I'm trying to do is to figure out what it is about you that yanks my chain."

"E-excuse me?"

"It's the damnedest thing," Sully said, recognizing it himself for the first time. "I don't trust you. I'm not sure I like you. You remind me too much of myself. You got an edge, Jessie."

"My name is Jessica. Try to remember it. Now why don't you move . . . before I cut your heart out."

That slow smile she was beginning to hate eased over his face. "Oh, it's too late for that. I don't have a heart."

"Is that a fact?"

"Practically a fact."

"Thanks for the warning. I'll aim lower."

"Jessie, girl, you've got a wicked mouth."

"Is that a crime too?" Her voice came out little more than a bedroom whisper.

"Oh, no. That is definitely not a crime."

She'd never heard so much approval in one sentence. In an instant the antagonism between them dissipated, replaced by an unbearable tension . . . anticipation. Her lips felt suddenly dry, and she had to fight the effort to wet them with her tongue. That would be an invitation to disaster, an invitation to be kissed.

As Sully lowered his head, she realized her mistake. Men like Sully never waited for invitations, which was why she'd always avoided them.

"Darlin'—" His lips were almost on hers. "The only crime would be letting a mouth like yours go to waste."

FIVE

Soft.

Her lips were so soft, Sully thought. No lipstick; just Jessie. Nothing between them, and everything between them. Sully touched his tongue along her bottom lip, testing her resistance, promising her pleasure. Promising himself pleasure.

When she opened her mouth beneath his, satisfaction flooded through his body, a surge of possessiveness at the simple acceptance. He hadn't expected Jessie to give herself up. He had expected her to keep her distance, to pull away like she had last night.

Deepening the kiss, he shoved the schedule in his back pocket and buried his fingers in her hair, cradling her head. Her mouth wasn't wicked at all, he discovered. There was a sweetness and an innocence that blew him away. It was so completely at odds with the woman she pretended to be.

He'd taken more than his share of kisses in thirty-four years, but never one like this. Never one that wrapped itself around his soul so completely. Never one that felt brand-new and just for him. Never one that threatened his self-control.

That's what kissing Jessie did. Right now he wanted to forget all the reasons he didn't trust her. He didn't care if this was the wrong time, the wrong place, and the wrong woman. Kissing her was the only thing that had felt right in longer than he could remember.

He moved closer until only a whisper of space existed between them, teasing them. Jessie's hands crept up his chest. Without taking his mouth from hers, he let his hands slide down her neck and catch her shoulders. He turned her and pressed her hard against one wall. As his tongue explored her mouth, he slowly laid his lower body against hers.

As Jessie shifted her hips to accommodate him, his arousal stroked her intimately. He could feel the tension building in her, the little shudder that she tried to control, but Sully wanted more. He wanted to hear her moan with the same frustration he felt.

He took her arms by the wrists, and pinned them to the wall with his hands, leaving her vulnerable. Her breasts brushed his shirt and teased him until he finally settled his chest against hers, letting himself enjoy every inch of her as he sank into her softness.

Jessica couldn't think clearly. All she could do was feel. Everything was forgotten as Sully seduced her with his mouth. The world narrowed to the scrape of his tongue against hers, the weight of his body molded to hers. By the time she remembered the derringer, it was already too late. Sully had jerked his mouth from hers as if she'd stung him.

"What the hell?" he hissed. When she struggled to loosen her arms, he tightened his grip. "I don't think so. Not yet. Not until I see what we've got here."

He brought her arms down, dragging them behind

her and holding her wrists with one hand. The whole procedure was quick and fluid—she assumed his expertise came from years of practice at subduing suspects. With the other hand he began to unbutton her top. She guessed his facility at this particular job was also due to years of practice.

Not bothering to argue or struggle, Jessica stood perfectly still and let him do what he wanted. If she struggled against him as he unbuttoned her blouse, he'd simply add resisting arrest to the impending charge of carrying a concealed weapon. They were alone; he was the cop. And he wasn't even sure he liked her. If he liked her, he would have just reached in and dragged the gun out. Doing it this way was to push her buttons. Literally.

Her options were limited at best. Lying to him wasn't going to do any good.

Telling him the truth wasn't going to slow him down either. Not now.

He was a man with a mission. He wouldn't believe her anyway. She'd done a fine job of damning herself. She called herself a fool for allowing Sullivan Kincaid past her defenses. Fools usually paid a price for stupidity; this was hers. He had the proverbial "smoking gun," or would have soon enough.

Except for the coldness in his eyes as he caught and held her gaze, she wouldn't have known how angry he was. His fingers weren't harsh or cruel. Oh no, his touch was gentle, seductive even as he lingered over each of the buttons. The back of his hand brushed against her flesh too often for it to be an accident.

And all the time he stared at her, pushing her, daring her to explain the derringer away before he uncovered it. She didn't. The game was over, and he'd won. Before they were done she'd have more important things to explain away than the weapon. She wasn't about to waste her breath on the small stuff.

The silence around them was so complete that she could hear the fabric buttons grate against the tight buttonholes as they popped free. Jessica refused to close her eyes as his fingers reached the last button, but she did stare at the ceiling. She gritted her teeth against the feel of his knuckles rubbing against her midriff.

When Sully finished, he spread her shirt open in two quick sweeps of his hand. She imagined him looking down for the first time. Envisioned the expression on his face as he saw the derringer stashed in her cleavage.

The idea that tortured her most was her absolute certainty that those incredible blue eyes took their sweet time as they roamed over her bra-covered breasts. Suddenly Jessica felt her nipples harden as the air-conditioning conspired against her to create a chill in the office. At least that's what she told herself. The other explanation was unthinkable.

"Well, well . . . what have we got here?" he mused finally. "A cross-your-heart-and-hope-to-die bra?"

Sully's joke fell on deaf ears. He didn't expect a snappy answer. Didn't really want one, but he needed the time to think. Truth be told, his mouth had gone dry the moment he dropped his gaze to her breasts. Jessie's bra was all but transparent. Her nipples were clearly defined and . . . perky. Sully swallowed. Ah damn, were they ever perky and begging for attention he itched to provide.

But there was the little problem of the gun. And the lies. And Phil Munro.

The fog of lust that had clouded his judgment and

blunted his instincts cleared as he stared at the small silver derringer nestled between her breasts. Some sort of elastic or Velcro sling obviously held the barrel and trigger guard in place. Only the edge of the grip peeked above the center of her bra.

Her chest wasn't exactly heaving, but her breathing was spectacularly erratic. Each breath rose and fell in an odd cadence that poorly imitated controlled breathing. Well, he allowed truthfully, it indicated her *attempt* to take long deep, smooth breaths of air. But all that careful control only served to amplify a chest that needed no amplification.

Sully decided a moment of silence was in order.

The quiet inspection began to grate on Jessica's nerves. When Sully didn't get it over with, she forced her eyes down and snapped, "What's the matter? You've never seen a gun before?"

"Lady," he said as he redirected his eyes to the derringer, "that's not a gun. That's a peashooter."

"Yeah, well, it shoots hollow point peas."

Sully raised an eyebrow but not his eyes. "I am impressed . . . but not by the toy gun."

Horrified, Jessica felt the heat of a blush rise to her face and prayed it hadn't started at her chest. But she knew it had. To make matters worse, she was beginning to lose the ability to distance herself. He had a way of dragging her back into the moment, back to the unexpected chemistry that existed between them.

Sully could affect her with a simple sentence, and she didn't like it. Somehow that felt more like a violation than the search, than being exposed. But she'd be damned if she let him know he could get to her. She'd spent her life making sure no one got close enough to slip inside her defenses. Wishing for the moon was dangerous. Weakness was vulnerability. She couldn't afford either of those.

She'd made a mistake with Sully, and she was about to correct it.

Forcing herself to remain pliant in his grasp, she let coldness seep into her words and into her eyes. "How delightful, but impressing you is not a life's ambition for me. So why don't you take the gun and let me go? While you're busy drooling and being impressed, I could catch my death of cold."

"Darlin', looking like that you could catch the Dallas Cowboys." He smiled and drew the derringer from between her breasts without letting her arms go. When he slipped it in his back pocket, he added, "I think you look healthy enough to fight off a chill or two while I check for other weapons."

She bit her tongue, refusing to rise to the bait. This was a game with him. He patted her down with his free hand. He didn't actually pat; he stroked, slow as molasses. Jessica trembled with the effort to control her anger. The search was purposeful, deliberate, and intended to shake her. The man knew exactly how to get to her.

Threats, raising his voice, rough handling . . . none of that would have fazed her, and he knew it. He wanted her off balance. He wanted the truth any way he could get it. The man was a bloodhound, and he'd sniffed out her lies before she'd ever told them. Now that he had concrete proof of his suspicions he wasn't going to let this go. All good cops were like that. Part bloodhound, part hellhound.

Jessica decided Sully was more one than the other.

When he was satisfied she was clean, he let her go. "Now you want to tell me who you are and why you carry the peashooter? And don't tell me it's for self-defense. I'm getting real tired of bein' lied to. Or would you rather wait until I run you through the computer?" He tapped his pocket. "You do have a license for this, don't you?"

Jessica narrowed her eyes and pulled her shirt together with as much dignity as she could muster. Her shoulders hurt from being pinned back. Refusing to let Sully rattle her, she shook off the ache and fastened every button before she answered. "I carry it for the same reason you carry your weapon. I might need it."

"For what?"

"Shooting two-legged rats."

Sully didn't like what he heard or what he saw in her eyes. She wasn't joking, and yet she couldn't possibly be serious. With a careless air she swung her hair forward and finger-combed the tangles from it.

"Shot many lately, have you?" he asked.

"No. Not a one." Her dark gaze never wavered from his. She never hesitated. The swiftness of her answer should have placated him. It didn't.

"Who are you, Jessie?"

He thought she wasn't going to answer. Finally she told him, "Why don't you ask Iris?"

"Now there's a fine idea."

A few seconds later he'd ushered Iris in and stood behind her, hands on the girl's shoulders. Iris had on purple biker shorts with lace eyelet trim and an incredibly loud tie-dyed T-shirt. Kid clothes on an old soul. After Iris looked expectantly at Sully and then at Jessica, she asked, "Are we in trouble again?"

"Just me. Tell him."

"Tell him what?"

"The truth."

"But we already told him the truth."

Jessica shook her head and smiled in spite of herself. Iris was a trooper, loyal to the end. "No, it's time for the 'truth truth.' The gig's up. If I'm not mistaken, Detective Kincaid thinks I've done something with your father."

Appalled, Iris turned to Sully. "She didn't know anything about Daddy being missing. Not until I called her."

"You didn't talk to Phil Munro yesterday?" Sully fired the question at Jessica like a missile.

"No. I haven't talked to Phil for a very long time."

"Why'd you lie?"

"Isn't that obvious? I didn't want to create an unnecessary panic. Iris could've been overreacting."

"About what?" His attention returned to Iris, who fiddled with her harmony ball as she answered.

"Daddy calls every Sunday if he's out of town. He didn't call this week. He always calls." She looked up then. She was biting her lip.

"Always?" Sully asked. "Never misses? Ever?"

Iris shook her head. "No, sir. There's no special time, but he calls on Sunday. Always."

Frowning, Sully considered the situation for a moment. Then he looked sharply at Jessica. "He's almost forty-eight hours overdue."

"I know."

"I don't like it."

"Iris and I weren't real happy about it either. I was going to give him until tomorrow." When his eyes narrowed, she quietly added, "I *would* have called you tomorrow."

"And in the meantime you thought you'd do a little investigating yourself."

"I thought I might."

"Who are you, Jessica? And where'd you come from?"

Iris spoke up as she crossed the room to be with Jessica. "She's one of Daddy's special bodyguards. There're just a few of them."

"I'm retired," Jessica answered. "Have been for a couple of years."

"Daddy still keeps her name on a list of his best. She came back because I called her."

"Before or after you called the police?" Sully asked.

"After."

"She was very busy on the phone. It seems I was Goldilocks's third choice. She called the CIA first," added Jessica helpfully, a deadpan expression on her face.

Suddenly Sully felt the sickening thud of trouble as it settled on his shoulders. "I don't think I want to hear this."

"Oh, but you must," Jessica echoed his earlier statement to her. "You want to make a federal case out of this. Then let's do it right. Let's get all the facts on the table."

"I was trying to find my dad," Iris explained.

"So," Jessica continued as if what followed was the most natural thing in the world, "she pushed the redial button on the phone in his bedroom at the beach house."

"And got the CIA?"

"We assume." She pulled Iris to her. Gone was any trace of insecurity or emotion. She was tough again, having slipped back into the role of Iris's protector. "The area code fits. They answered the phone with some top secret spy jargon garbage and when she couldn't identify herself in the accepted manner, they freaked."

"I didn't like 'em anyway." Iris crossed her arms in

that weird way kids had of holding their elbows. "They were cold. I don't think they care about my dad."

Sully paced a few steps, rubbing the back of his neck. "What does Munro Security or Phil Munro have to do with the CIA?"

Iris shrugged. Jessica simply stared at him, silently suggesting that they'd all be better off if they didn't know the answer to that question.

"Okay, we'll put that issue aside for the moment. Is that all you've got to go on?" He looked at them, his hands on his hips.

"That's all the facts."

Once again Sully was struck by the notion that it was a damn shame that Jessica was so slippery. Despite concrete evidence that the woman wasn't nearly as innocent as her kiss pretended, he still wanted her. That surprised the hell out of him. He liked his women straightforward and uncomplicated. Jessica was anything but.

She'd given up lying, but the half-truths were just as bad. She was very good at it. Fortunately, he was better.

"Good," he finally said. "Now let's start on the non-facts. Let's start with what worries you, Jessica."

The black book and that file. But she couldn't say that out loud. Not to Sully. Not to anyone. "We can't prove it, but we think someone's broken in to the beach house. Phil's office door was open, and he's the only one with the key. The place looked *gone through.* Some of the pages of his calendar were missing."

Sully reached into his back pocket and pulled out the page she'd had when he walked in. "So you came down here to check this calendar." He glanced down at the calendar sheet, at the words she'd already memorized.

Gemini Electronics. 3274 Petrie.

"Why this page?"

"It was Friday's page, and it's the only one with an address." That was the truth, but she'd have taken that page regardless of how many appointments existed on Phil's calendar.

She smiled when Sully strode to the desk to check. He didn't trust her. Smart man. While he flipped pages, Jessica studied Iris, wondering how she was holding up. It was one thing to *think* your dad was missing and another to have that suspicion confirmed by the actions of a police detective.

After Sully tore two more pages out of Phil's calendar, he picked up the phone and called Jericho. A brief phone conversation later, he said, "Let's go."

"Where?"

"Gemini Electronics. You wanted to investigate, so here's your chance."

"Do we have a choice?"

"Yeah." He stopped beside them. "We can swing by my old squad room instead, and ask someone to run your name and the gun through the computer."

"We'll go with you."

"I thought so," Sully said, and put his hand on the small of her back to urge her toward the door.

The polite gesture caught them both by surprise. Because of her crop top, his hand rested in the small of her bare back. His touch created a focal point of heat, an intimate contact reminding them of what happened between them. She managed to swallow the gasp before it came out and arched her back away from his touch, but not quickly enough. The heat remained. Like a brand, his imprint.

After clearing her throat, she said, "Let's go, Iris." They were almost to the parking lot, Iris dashing ahead of them, when she remembered to ask him, "Your *old* squad room?"

"Houston PD. Twelve years."

"That explains it."

"What?"

"Why you don't act like a small-town cop."

"I didn't realize it showed."

"Only when you walk, talk, or breathe. Let me guess. You were undercover narcotics? You've got that just-crazy-enough gleam in your eyes and enough don't-mess-with-me swagger to get along in that world."

"No. I did my time in the major case squad." He frowned when he said it, as if a shadow fell over him at the memories. Sully looked directly at her, his gaze boring into hers, almost warning her. "I was very good. Not everyone can do it. You have to think like a serial killer, like a kidnapper. Like evil."

"H-how . . . ?" She was unsure how to ask what she wanted to know, but he told her anyway.

"It's easy. All you have to do is give yourself up to the darkness. Crawl inside their skin."

A chill swept through Jessica, and the sun couldn't warm her. It couldn't reach the icy spot in her soul. She understood all about the darkness. "Why did you walk away?"

He didn't answer; she didn't ask again. She was suddenly terrified of what the answer might be.

The three of them sat in the front seat of Sully's car. Iris didn't mind being in the middle. Especially now that the flip-flop feeling in the pit of her stomach was getting worse. She didn't want to be alone in the back. That's where she was headed before Jessica pulled her out by grabbing the hem of her T-shirt and directing her to the front.

Sully didn't seem to mind, but then he hadn't said much of anything since he'd told her to buckle up. As they approached the turn for Petrie, Iris leaned forward as far as she could. Gripping the dash, she focused on the distance. "What's the address?"

Sully slid the calendar page, which lay in front of him, toward her. "Thirty-two seventy-four. Gemini Electronics."

Slowly Iris took the sheet and stared at it. The word "gemini" shouted at her. It couldn't be; she didn't want it to be. But there it was. She held out the sheet to Jessica, searching her face for reassurance.

Gemini was Jessica Dannemora's code word.

Jessica had hoped Iris didn't know or wouldn't pick up on the word that had struck her so forcefully when she flipped through Phil's calendar. At a loss for how to convey to Iris that the name was a coincidence without tipping Sully, Jessica finally shook her head the tiniest bit. Then the girl quietly held out her right hand. Iris believed in all that mumbo jumbo about vibrations and auras. She wanted to test Jessica.

Slowly Jessica eased her hand toward the small waiting one. As Iris wrapped her fingers around it, she closed her eyes. After what seemed like an eternity, she nodded and opened them. But she didn't let go.

Letting out the breath she'd been holding, Jessica realized that she'd wanted to pass that test more than she cared to admit. She wanted someone to trust her unconditionally. She wanted a connection that didn't rely on words or actions. Pain seared her as she realized what she really wanted, what she'd refused to voice for so many years now. She wanted Jenny back. She wanted to be whole again.

Unfamiliar tears blurred her sight as she stared at the small hand wrapped around hers. Blinking, she cleared her vision and then cursed Sully. All this damned emotion was his fault. He'd started it with that seduction of his. Rampant hormones were screwing up the precarious balance that kept her sane.

Not feeling anything was so much easier.

When she looked up, Sully was slowing the car. The street had dissolved into a collection of dead and dying businesses. For every two storefronts or buildings that were occupied, another was boarded up. Cigarette wrappers, fast-food bags, and broken beer bottles littered the curb, even in front of the viable businesses. No one seemed to care about the character of the neighborhood.

Finally stopping the car alongside a vacant lot, Sully announced, "As close as I can figure it, this is our address."

"We're looking for an electronics company. This can't be it."

Pointing first at the side of the lot behind them and then at the other before them, he said, "Thirty-two seventy-two and thirty-two seventy-six."

Slowly Jessica became aware of the pressure on her hand, and looked down at Iris. The girl's attention was riveted across the street. She shifted for a better view.

As she did, Iris clutched her hand even harder and shakily whispered, "I think that's my dad's car."

Jessica's heart stopped and lurched onward again. A shiny black Mercedes had been stripped, the victim of urban warfare. Instinctively her arm went around Iris and her eyes sought Sully. This time she was looking for some reassurance.

His face was expressionless, and he already had the radio in his hand. When he got through to dispatch and identified himself and his location, he said, "We're going to need a crime scene unit out here."

SIX

"*Dammit, Kincaid!* Get in here!"

A number of detectives in the Houston squad room jumped nervously, but his former captain's explosion came as no surprise to Sullivan Kincaid. Nor did it upset Jessica. She sat beside Iris, holding the girl's hand, legs crossed at the knee, impassive—just as remote with him as she'd been before the kiss. The only emotional chink in her armor since the kiss had been that split second she'd turned to him after they found the Mercedes.

Suddenly the need to shake, rattle, and roll Jessica Daniels came roaring back, just as strong as it had been that first night. And that was not good. The need to shake her out of her emotional distance would lead him down roads he couldn't afford to travel, like the scene in Munro's office. It was a game of control that would only escalate. The need to force a reaction from her would only bring out the worst in him.

Like father, like son. So he'd made a habit of avoiding women who got to him on anything more than a sexual level. He shook his head unhappily. Some habits just weren't meant to be broken.

"*Kincaid!*" his old boss hollered for the second time.

Sully dragged his mind away from Jessica and sighed the sigh of a condemned man. It was time to face the music. This particular butt-chewing had been inevitable from the moment he'd called in the crime scene unit. Ancient metal castors squealed a protest as he pushed the chair away from the vacant desk he'd occupied since giving his statement.

Peter Keelyn, the last in the long line of partners Sully'd had over the years, looked his way and offered condolences. "If you don't survive this, I want you to know . . . I'll take good care of your lady and that sweet chrome forty-five."

The undeniable stab of possession he felt toward Jessica shook Sully. He didn't crack a smile as he walked past and said, "Now, why would I leave you anything, Peter? I don't even like you."

"Hey, man, you can't take it with you."

"Sure I can," he called over his shoulder. "I cut a deal with the devil."

"Hell, Sully, you are the devil."

"That's what my daddy always said." *And that was on a good day.*

Without bothering to straighten his tie, he strode into Captain Harlan Robertson's office. A neatly knotted tie wasn't going to make much of a dent in the man's displeasure. An apologetic hangdog attitude might help, but Sully had never been able to manage "hangdog" with any degree of sincerity. And Harlan knew him much too well to fall for an act.

"Close the door."

"Yes, sir." Sully obliged by snagging it with the

heel of his cowboy boot and kicking it shut behind him. The old-fashioned metal venetian blinds covering the window to the squad room rattled as the door made contact with the jamb.

Sully's gaze never wavered from the man who had not only been his captain, but was also one of the few people he trusted enough to call friend. Not that they let anything so trivial as a friendship get in the way of business. His former boss was the only one who knew the real reason Sully walked away from the major case unit.

Harlan looked about as healthy as an emaciated marathon runner. Even the starch in his shirts couldn't keep the fabric from hanging on his spare frame. Like the rest of his body, Harlan's lips were thin, narrowing to a faint line when he was unhappy.

At the moment, Sully decided his old boss must be downright despondent. His lips had disappeared completely.

Before he began, Harlan flicked his eyes at one of the two chairs in his office—a silent command. Sully sat, leaned back, and rested an ankle over his knee. Obviously dispensing with formalities, Harlan swore and then got right to the point.

"Sully, you are supposed to be handing out jay-walking tickets in Jericho and not knee-deep in missing persons. Why are you back in my town?"

"Sight-seeing?" Sully casually shifted a little more to the right and laced his fingers across his abdomen. When Harlan didn't smile, Sully said, "Someone's got to catch the bad guys."

"It doesn't always have to be you."

"Why don't you tell that to the bad guys? I didn't pick this case. It picked me. I gotta tell you, Harlan, this one makes me nervous. The truth is, it makes me more than a little nervous. I've got one of those feelings."

"Oh, Jesus," Harlan whispered and reached for the aspirin bottle on the credenza behind him. Unfortunately, Sully's intuition was legendary. So Harlan slugged three of them down and leaned back in his chair, closing his eyes as if he could picture a hundred horrible scenarios and a million complications. Then he opened his eyes and swore several times. "I don't need this. Not now."

"I didn't exactly ask for it myself."

His friend gave him a long-suffering look that implied otherwise. "Like hell. What do we have?"

"We got a stripped car belonging to millionaire Phil Munro, who missed a scheduled call to his kid on Sunday, and a female bodyguard type who I think is lying to me every time she opens her mouth."

"Why should you be surprised that women lie to you? If there's an amoral woman within earshot, she makes a beeline for you. Explain that to me. Why *is* that?"

"Safety in numbers?" Sully deadpanned.

The captain in Harlan did not appreciate the humor. He never did. Rubbing his eyes, he sighed long and hard. "Best guess on Munro."

"Drove there for a meeting. Confirmed by calendar notes. Either went willingly with someone else to another location or they waited until he was out of the Mercedes to pop him. There's no sign of struggle in the car. No blood. Nothing outside the car either. Given Munro's background, we have to figure he was more than capable of defending himself. I can't imagine him going down easy. So whatever happened, I don't think it happened on Petrie."

"Ransom demands?"

"None yet. But I told you. I don't trust the woman. We don't communicate real well."

"You never do."

"Yeah, well, I usually don't have to disarm 'em. This one carries a derringer in her bra."

"In her bra? How would you know that?" For a moment, Harlan froze, staring at Sully as if contemplating murder. "Tell me you aren't intimate with her. You better damn well tell me you aren't."

Shrugging, Sully told him, "Okay. Have it your way. I'm not. Well, technically not."

"Give me a reason."

"For disarming her?" Sully purposely misunderstood the question. "I have this little rule about being the only one in the room with a gun."

"No! You tell me why *you* had to be the one involved in this. You couldn't have made a simple phone call to us? A little 'heads up' on the playground?"

"I'm funny that way." Sully leaned forward, finally angry himself. "When smoke alarms go off, I don't take the batteries out, call the fire department, and forget it. I keep looking for smoke. And lookee here . . . I found a fire."

"You always do. Looking for fires is a problem with you, isn't it, Sully? You're always looking for someone to hate more than yourself, and we both know it."

Sully stood up and flattened his palms on Harlan's desk. All the trappings of professional courtesy were gone. All formality stripped away as two old friends covered familiar ground. "We don't want to do this again."

"No, *you* don't want to do this again." Harlan stood up for the first time. Even so, he was still inches short of looking Sully in the eye. But that didn't seem to faze him. Harlan was one of only two people Sully had never been able to subdue with a stare. Jessie was the other.

The older man continued without missing a beat. "You wanted out of Houston, out of the *badlands*? You wanted to back away from the edge before you lost your ability to feel anything but hate? To tell the good guys from the bad guys? I'm going to give you some advice. Hell, no. I'm going to give you an order. You live with that decision, Sully! It was a *by God* good one. Exorcise your own demons and leave the bad guys to us. This isn't your case."

"These bad guys are messin' in my backyard," Sully pointed out, his voice soft with suppressed anger. "Munro has a summer house on Jericho. His little girl lives there. I found the car." Sully pulled back from the desk. "I'm on it."

"Give me three minutes to call your chief, and you won't be. Munro's primary residence is here. Munro Security is here. The car—the evidence of foul play—is here. This one's ours. Peter's on it."

For a long moment they stared at each other, silence reigning. Sully reached for the doorknob, uncertain whether his anger was territorial or whether it came from the realization that everything Harlan said was true. Finally he jerked open the door. "Peter better be on top of it. You tell him."

"You tell him," Harlan fired back. "And then you take that little girl home, make sure she's safe, give 'em the standard speech, and you let us do our job. We'll let you know when and if you can assist."

"Would that be when hell freezes over?"

"That'd be a precise estimate." Harlan sat back down. "We got your statements. Now get out of here. I'll be in touch with your chief."

Jessica pulled Iris to her feet the moment Sully blew back into the squad room. There was really no other way to describe it. Whatever happened in the captain's office had changed him. Sully was always dangerous, even when he smiled. But this was different.

It was as if something had stripped him down to his essence. There was no light to balance the dark. There was no cocky smile, no silken threat. Instead, the threat was raw and real, barely contained.

When he looked at her, the hair on the back of her neck stood up. God help anyone who crossed Sullivan Kincaid. Unbidden, another thought came to her. God help any woman who loved the man. Loving him would be like holding a lightning rod in a thunderstorm and hoping it wouldn't hurt.

"Are we done?" she asked quietly.

"Almost." He turned away to catch the attention of the detective who'd taken their statements. "Peter, Harlan says you're the lead on this one. Do me a favor. You turn over every rock. Ask every question twice, and you do it fast. You understand?"

Instead of taking offense at Sully's high-handed tone, Peter visibly paled. "A feeling?"

Sully didn't answer. He took Jessica's arm and walked away.

Halfway down the corridor, Iris said, "I thought you didn't have feelings."

Sully never broke stride. "Sometimes I wish I didn't."

"Me too," Iris agreed.

Looking first at Iris and then at the man who dragged her inexorably through the station, Jessica realized that they were talking about two different things. And she agreed with them both.

Feelings exacted too high a price on the soul. That's why she'd closed herself off after Jenny was killed. It was the only way she could make it. Pain she could control, even the loneliness, but the guilt for surviving built up inside her no matter what she did. When Phil Munro found her and offered her a way to channel that guilt, she grabbed the chance.

An eye for an eye. A life for a life.

But all she'd done was trade one hell for another. No matter that her sanctioned targets hurt people . . . hurt children. No matter that they tortured people, and had to be stopped. She was still in hell.

When she realized she was becoming—had already become—what she hated, she walked away. No, not walked. Ran. She ran as hard as she could from reality and the sanctimonious justifications, hiding herself away like some hermit. For a year she'd managed to shut down and keep the feelings at bay. The second year of her retirement, the nightmares had returned.

Nothing she could do seemed to stop them. Sully and Iris were only going to make it worse. Nerves that had been deadened from neglect were beginning to tingle.

Right now, she wanted to stop the process before it was too late. She didn't want to worry about Phil. She didn't want to be responsible for Iris. She didn't want to need the strength she found in Sully's strong hand wrapped around her arm, supporting her. Most of all she didn't want to remember how it felt to be kissed by the man.

All she wanted was to be left alone on her little piece of land in the middle of the Texas hill country. That was God's country and the closest to grace she'd been in a long time. The closest she would probably ever be.

As Sully dragged her into the late-afternoon sunlight, the concrete and granite pulsed heat. But none of it held a candle to the heat Sully generated with that one touch on her arm. Fighting the heat was the only way to keep her emotions cold.

The drive back to the Munro complex was too short and too long. Iris slumped against her, another spot of warmth. A spot that Jessica couldn't find it within herself to fight against.

Iris had said almost nothing since they'd left the station, but she'd asked a hundred questions earlier. Some of them over and over until she finally accepted that no one knew the answers. Her eyes were completely dry. Jessica didn't know if that was bad or good. Bad more than likely.

"When we get your car," Sully said, his words landing powerfully in the silence, "I need to run inside the offices long enough to use the phone. I'll need to call Jericho and check in."

Iris stiffened at his words. "We have to go up to Daddy's office."

Sully glanced sideways. "Why?"

"I want our picture. It's the one from Easter. It's on his desk. I want it." Her chin was set, and those unshed tears which had worried Jessica bubbled to the surface, but not yet spilling.

"Okay." Jessica didn't hesitate. Not because she wanted another chance to rummage through Phil's desk for the file and book, but because erasing the despair in Iris's expression was suddenly important. "We'll get it while Sully makes his call."

"I'll go up with you," Sully said, "and make the call

from Phil's office." His tone was casual, but his expression wasn't.

Jessica pressed her lips together. The whole damn world knew about Phil's disappearance now. The "secret" was out, and yet he still didn't trust her. *Do you really expect him to? He found a gun in your bra.*

The memory brought a rush of heat to her face. Quickly followed by a rush of apprehension in her stomach. Sully hadn't given the derringer to the other detective or, to her knowledge, asked anyone to run the serial number or check for a permit. The officer who took her statement seemed willing to accept her story of Iris's phone call, seemed to believe that Jessica Daniels was no more than a dear family friend, coming to soothe a worried child.

Sully didn't seem nearly so willing to believe her role was innocent. Yet he kept silent about the gun, didn't voice his suspicions in the squad room. He had his own agenda, just as she had hers. Both of them scrambling in the dark for the advantage.

"No problem," she agreed. "We'll all go together."

And they did, almost in lockstep. By the time they reached the tenth floor, Jessica wanted to scream. Sully's presence smothered her—fingertips at the small of her back to urge her through doorways, into the elevator, out of the elevator. It was her preoccupation with him that caused her carelessness.

She was in such a hurry to get away from him, she plowed right into two gentlemen carrying overloaded cardboard file boxes. Catching one of the lids before it slid off, Jessica opened her mouth to spit out the reflex apology, but it died on her lips as she got an eyeful. Nondescript dark suits, generic ties, average height, average build. Everything about them was one hundred percent government issue. These were company men; she'd stake her life on it.

Looking at the bulging boxes and knowing they might have the names, all she could think of was that they'd make her kill again. They wouldn't let her go. And she couldn't be a part of that. Not again. She'd made a deal with Phil, but these men wouldn't honor it.

With a smile that she knew was off center and as fake as they come, she backed up into Sully, hard enough that he had to circle her waist and steady her. "Oh, my," she said, recovering her voice. "I've almost knocked everyone down. I'm so sorry."

The two men stared wordlessly at them, obviously waiting for the trio to move away from the front of the elevator. Sully obliged by steering Iris behind him and drawing Jessica to one side, his arm still around her waist. He was also careful to keep his front toward the men so that the gun holstered at the small of his back was hidden. Instinct told Sully that broadcasting his status as a cop to these two would be a mistake.

The elevator whooshed open as soon as they pushed the button with the corner of one of the boxes. Sully nodded his head as they got in and gave them a big ol' Texas good-neighbor smile. The men stood motionless, creating a tableau as the elevator doors closed. Everyone seemed frozen in place, even Iris.

"Who were they?" she finally whispered when the soft ding of the elevator shook them out of their trance.

An angry and unfamiliar female voice answered them. "The government. They came swooping in here right after lunch and ransacked Mr. Munro's office. Taking whatever they wanted." She huffed unhappily. "Something about a national security matter. They said they'd bring it all back, but Mr. Munro's not going to like this. Iris, honey, I'm glad you're here. Do you know where your daddy is? I've got to talk to him. And fast."

All three heads had swiveled toward her the moment the woman spoke. She was fortyish and ready for battle, hands on her size twelve hips and her size five fuchsia pumps planted squarely in the beige carpet. Jessica recognized her immediately, but the woman's gaze seemed to brush past her to rivet on Sully as if he was the real threat.

"I'm Carol McMillian. Phil Munro's secretary."

"Sullivan Kincaid."

That jolted her. "The detective who called yesterday?"

"Yes, ma'am."

"Something happened." It wasn't a question.

"Yes, ma'am."

Carol was silent for a moment as she absorbed the news, almost like a widow whose brain refused to process information. Then her eyes flicked over the woman backed up against him, over his hand which was still flattened protectively on her midriff. Very slowly, he moved his hand and stepped away from her. The fact that Jessica hadn't already withdrawn from his touch was filed in his brain for examination another time. And so was the feel of soft skin beneath his palm and fingers.

"Mr. Munro's car was found abandoned," he announced, dropping the news on the woman like a house from Kansas. "Stripped for parts."

She blanched. "Was he—?"

"No." Sully cut her off. "There's no evidence of foul play beyond the fact that his car was vandalized. The Houston police have taken over the case."

"Completely?" The surprised question was from Jessica.

Sully ignored her. "Until the officers come by to interview you, Ms. McMillian, I'd appreciate it if you said nothing to the other employees. Not about the men who were just here or about the car being found."

She nodded, still slightly dazed, uncertain what to do next.

"Iris wants a picture from her dad's office," Jessica murmured into the silence, and the woman nodded again. Sully mentioned the phone call and excused himself too.

The entire length of the corridor, Jessica felt Sully's eyes boring into her back. She knew he followed only a few steps behind, waiting for her to make a mistake. She could sense the patience in him, the watchfulness.

Regardless of his statement that Houston had taken over the investigation, he'd be asking questions soon. He might have been replaced in an official capacity, but Sully wasn't the kind of man to let someone else clean up his mess. His first questions would no doubt be about the CIA guys and her reaction to them.

Jessica cringed mentally at her lapse of control. She hadn't expected them to be so bold as to march into Phil's company office and haul off files in broad daylight. There'd been no way to disguise the sick tension that had tightened her stomach muscles. Every bit of the fear had been transmitted right to Sully through the contact of his hand, of his chest against her back. Sully had known immediately that something was wrong. He'd followed her lead and played the innocent bystander, but now he'd want explanations.

Out of the frying pan and into the fire. Explanations were the most dangerous of all.

Reaching Phil's office seemed like a milestone, a chance to escape Sully's intense scrutiny, but it wasn't. He caught her just beyond the door and held her back with the softest of touches on her shoulder as Iris went to the desk. Together they stood slightly to the right of the doorway, surveying the room around them. All of the pictures were off the walls. Several drawers of the cherry credenza-style file cabinets lining one side were open and obviously gutted of important files. She imagined the drawers of Phil's desk had fared no better.

Silently she cursed Sully for interrupting her first search of the office. Now it was too late. If the file or the book had been here . . .

Sully leaned closer, eerily finishing her thoughts. "Whatever it was, it's gone now."

In spite of herself, Jessica rubbed the side of her neck against her shoulder, trying to erase the sensation that his breath created as it whispered across her skin. Her reaction weakened her disclaimer. "I don't know what you're talking about."

"Darlin', whatever it was you were looking for this morning is most likely in those boxes we just passed. Isn't it?" His voice was low, meant only for her. "The real question is, 'Do you think *they* know what they're looking for?'"

She didn't respond, but that was answer enough for a man like Sully. He took bits and pieces that most people would ignore and wove them into theories that were impossibly viable.

Iris got the photograph and turned toward them. "Can we go now? I don't want to stay here anymore."

"I'll take her down," Jessica volunteered. There was certainly nothing to keep her in the office now that the agents had come and gone. All she could do was hope.

Even so, she didn't move, waiting for Sully's agreement rather than walking out. It cost her nothing to pretend Sully was in control. And as long as he believed he was, he'd keep his suspicions to himself instead of sharing them with the Houston police. One smart man was quite enough to deal with. She didn't want to have to juggle an entire department.

"All right," he finally agreed. "But wait in the lobby. We'll caravan. I want to make sure you get back to Jericho."

"Make sure we get back?" Jessica echoed, unable to keep the trace of sarcasm out of her voice. "Where else would we go?"

"Twenty-two Knoll Road, Utopia, Texas, for starters."

Her hands stilled in the act of reaching for Iris's shoulders as she passed. *He already knew where she lived?* A half beat later she dropped her hands, sending Iris out the door to talk to Carol and wait by the elevator.

When they were alone, she said, "I thought you said you were off Phil's case."

"Yeah. But I'm not off yours." It was both a warning and a promise. The warning scared the hell out of her, and the promise took her breath away with the possibilities.

"How do you know my address? I never told you. You weren't there for my statement."

"Didn't need to be. I checked out the rental car this morning. Sloppy of you to leave the identifying paperwork on the dash last night. Anyone with a badge can get a copy of your driver's license information from the rental agency."

"Gee, Sully, looks like you went to a lot of trouble to find out where I live. Why didn't you just search my purse or ask me for my phone number?"

"That wouldn't be nearly as much fun, would it?"

"I don't know. Searching for the gun certainly seemed to amuse you. I'm surprised you didn't check my panties for my birth certificate while you were at it. But then, you weren't thinking very clearly at the time."

It was the wrong thing to say, and she knew it as soon as the words were out of her mouth. Taunting Sully was tantamount to prodding a sleeping lion. Her heart thudded sickeningly. She reminded herself that the door was still open. Nothing could happen. Nothing.

So why did it feel as if something *was* happening? Why was she *hoping* something would happen? His eyes burned into hers, relentless and angry.

Sully gritted his teeth as she flung that little barb at him. Ooh, the lady was good, reminding him that his self-control had gone right out the window this morning. She knew how to push buttons, but she was sadly mistaken if she thought all he could do was unfasten them. He could push 'em too.

"Don't you worry." Sully let his gaze travel downward until it rested where the juncture of her thighs was hidden beneath her skirt. "I've been givin' your panties a lot of thought."

As he intended, his plain talk shut her up. Her eyes flared with a mixture of what he thought was panic, anger, and maybe the tiniest twinge of arousal.

"Tread carefully, Jessie. The only reason I haven't turned you and that peashooter over to Houston PD is that girl trusts you and needs you right now. So I'm content to watch your little drama play out. But if you piss me off, I can change my mind in a New York instant."

"What?" she mocked, anger gaining the upper hand in her expression and voice. "And give up the only chance you have to stay on this case? Peddle that line of bull to someone who's going to buy it. I saw your expression when you walked out of the captain's office. He took you off the case. Face it, Sully, you're not givin' me up to them because I'm your ticket back into the game."

"You'd do well to remember that I'm the one who can punch your ticket."

"How can I forget with you glaring at me like that all the time? Why the hell are you so angry at me, Sully? What'd I do to you?"

"Besides the lying? The gun? The secrecy?"

"Yeah." She laughed. "Besides that. It's not enough. Not for this."

They hadn't raised their voices, but they were so close now, he could lean down and kiss her if he wanted. And he wanted to. He wanted to do more than kiss her. None of it was romantic or elegant or gentle. No hearts and flowers. Just sweat and satisfaction. All of it was erotic and gritty and rough.

"Why are you so angry?" she whispered, reminding him that she was waiting.

"You don't get it, do you?" Sully flicked his gaze at her mouth, exercising every ounce of control he had not to take it with his. Slowly he placed his fingers along the edge of her collarbone and used his thumb to stroke the hollow at the base of her throat. Her pulse jumped beneath his touch.

"Jessie, if I stop being angry, we're going to end up in bed. Or up against a wall. Leave my anger alone or there'll be hell to pay."

"Then I'm safe. I've already paid hell." If she hadn't been running—*escaping*—when she said it, Sully would have admired her comeback.

"Not like this," Sully said softly.

The phone call only took a few minutes. When he was done, he stopped by the secretary's desk and gave her his card. "Keep this just in case, Carol."

"Okay. And would you tell Miss Daniels I'm sorry I didn't speak to her? I feel awful for not recognizing her, but I was so agitated over those men and what they did to the office."

"That's right. I forgot. Miss Daniels is a former employee. How long has it been since she worked here?"

Startled, Carol said, "She never worked here. And I would know. I address all the Christmas cards every year. Mr. Munro has this thing about a personal holiday greeting for every employee. Her name's never been on the list."

"Then how do you know her?"

"She's an associate of Mr. Munro's. She's in the business or something. She used to come in a couple of times a year."

"Are you sure?" Sully's mind was already heaping the latest lie to the pile accumulating at Jessica's feet.

"That white streak in her hair is a little hard to forget." Carol sounded rock-solid on that point.

Sully asked to make another phone call. This one took a little longer because he had to dial information for the number, but he finally reached the Utopia police and identified himself.

SEVEN

As soon as Jessica pressed the code, the beach house gate drifted open on silent gears. She took her foot off the brake and pushed the accelerator. Neither the stop-and-start motion of the car or her second call to Iris produced more than a muffled grunt from the sleeping girl.

Jessica frowned, knowing that falling asleep had been more than Iris's way of dealing with the sun, which had hovered on their horizon most of the way back to Jericho. Iris had closed her eyes, not to shut out the piercing light coming through the window, but to shut out reality. It was an old trick, and not very effective. At least not for more than a few hours at a time.

Unfortunately everyone had to learn that for themselves. Iris would soon enough, and Jessica wondered why fate always felt the need to teach that particular lesson at such an early age. She also wondered why waxing philosophical gave her headaches.

Jessica rubbed her temple and drove to the front of the house, Sully right on her tail—as he had been the entire trip. She swore under her breath, tired of being chased and just plain tired. They hadn't left Houston until almost five o'clock. Between the long drive and stopping to get Iris some dinner, it was after seven.

And *still* plenty of day left, Jessica thought irritably.

In the odd way of daylight saving time and summer, twilight had abandoned the early evening, delaying the night. Ordinarily she worshiped the light and dreaded the dark. Night was a time for facing the past, a time for the nightmares.

Funny how perspectives changed so easily. After a day in Sully's company, she craved a little darkness in which to hide. Since the afternoon visit to Munro Security, Sully had grown icy, as if holding himself in check, but the anger was still there, smoldering, waiting to flame. With Iris between them, dinner had been neither the time nor the place to continue their last discussion. So they had maintained an uneasy truce, responding to innocuous questions with vague answers.

Dreading the next confrontation, Jessica climbed out of her car. There would be one. Of that she was sure. Although he hadn't grilled her yet, Sully wouldn't have forgotten the sober suits with boxes. Cops never forgot, and they never forgave. Especially not stubborn cops like Sully, ones who got the job done without excuses.

He was already out of his car, eating up the ground between them with long purposeful strides. Sully looked like a man with a few things on his mind and the newly found time to say them. As much to escape him as to wake Iris, Jessica started to lean back into the car. Sully stopped her, his voice reproachful.

"Let her sleep. The kid's wiped out." He

shrugged. "I've seen it before. It's the emotion. It'll be better if I carry her inside."

"She's too . . ." Before she could voice the objection, he was around the car and easing the door open. ". . . big," she finished lamely.

With one hand Sully kept Iris from tumbling out while he slid the other beneath her knees. In a smooth, quick movement, as easily as if she weighed no more than air, he had her out of the car and against his chest. Jessica realized the girl wasn't that big at all. Now that her eyes were closed and the perceptive watchfulness was hidden, she looked younger than twelve. She seemed fragile and innocent.

An unfamiliar and unfocused anger stabbed Jessica as she realized that Iris had spent her life relying on the kindness of strangers. An entourage of bodyguards, maids, and hit women didn't count for real companionship and guidance. What kind of family was that for a kid? None at all. Unfortunately that's all Iris had. And hope.

The kid wanted so badly for her father to be alive. Iris loved him, worshiped him. Jessica wasn't at all certain an absentee father like Phil Munro deserved her love. Money didn't matter to a kid like Iris. Neither did the houses, the cars, and the private schools.

None of it had ever mattered to Jessica. None of it could replace the gaping hole ripped out of her heart when she realized her own father had cared more about money than getting his daughters back alive. Whenever someone asked her what a life was worth, she could tell them to the penny. A quarter of a million dollars.

She'd pay ten times that much if it would bring Jenny back. But it wouldn't. Nothing could bring

Jenny back. There was no way she could ever make it right.

Jessica dragged her mind to the present as Sully turned to bump the door shut with his hip. She saw Iris's eyes fight against the drowsiness weighing them down. They fluttered open long enough to register Sully's face. At least that's what Jessica thought, but the stare was slightly off—more like over his shoulder than on his face.

"Good," Iris mumbled as her lids fell, and smiled at Sully. Her chin dipped toward her chest. "She stopped . . . crying."

Puzzled, Jessica wondered if she'd heard Iris correctly. Then she watched Sully's knees buckle—just for an instant. That was only an illusion of course. The man's knees wouldn't dare betray him. Nevertheless he appeared ill at ease, frozen in his tracks, frowning warily at the top of a head full of blond curls. As if he was afraid Iris might say something else. Something worse.

Jessica raised an eyebrow and shut the car door.

What do you know that I should know, Iris? Sound asleep and without even trying the girl had managed to shake Sully right down to his cowboy boots. Jessica found herself smiling. The man was human after all.

Before she could ask about the cryptic mumbling, Lincoln stepped outside. He looked every inch the bodyguard today. His impeccably starched shirt and saw grass-colored trousers were sharp enough to have been featured in *GQ* magazine, but the shoulder holster and 9mm Beretta were straight out of *Mercenary Monthly*.

Lincoln held the door for Sully, checking Iris carefully as she was carried by. "I was beginning to worry."

Trailing in Sully's wake, Jessica told him, "Don't

stop now, Linc. It looks like we may have plenty to worry about." Although she didn't have much hope, she asked, "Has Phil called?"

"No. No one has." That was a subtle reprimand. The next statement was a subtle request for information. "The police weren't with you when you left."

"Give us a minute, okay?" she asked, and tucked her hair behind her ears. "Iris doesn't need to hear this again."

Sully waited silently for her at the foot of the stairs. She brushed past and led him to Iris's room without a single hesitation. Making a mental blueprint of her surroundings was another old habit that had snapped into action last night. Iris had given her the nickel tour before they'd settled in for that long talk.

The room was cool and semidark. A welcome relief after the day's heat. Above twin beds were posters of unicorns and a road sign that said "Angel crossing." Jessica smiled, remembering her own preteen fascination with unicorns, and moved to one of the beds. She subdued the family of trolls inhabiting it—they looked more manageable than the explosion of clothes on the other bed. Then she shoved back the purple spread and stepped out of the way. For all Sully's rough handling of women, he was apparently also capable of gentleness. That was obvious as he put Iris down on the mattress. She landed so softly that she simply snuggled into the pillow and didn't move again. Not even when a lock of hair slipped down across her cheek to tease her nose.

Sully reached out to brush the hair away, his big hand making the girl's cheek look delicate by comparison. Abruptly, as if embarrassed to have been caught in a random act of kindness, he pulled his hand back and walked out of the room.

"Don't worry, Sully," she whispered as she followed him into the hallway, "I won't tell anybody you can actually be decent when you try."

"I don't imagine there are many people who'd believe you."

Bristling, Jessica said, "If that cutting little statement was supposed to be another insult—"

"No, Jessie." He laughed bitterly, shaking his head. "This time I was taking the knife to myself. 'Decent' isn't what most people expect out of Sullivan Kincaid."

"Then what do they expect?"

He turned and blocked her path down the stairs. "I wouldn't know. I don't ask them."

The grim set of his jaw convinced her he did know *exactly* what people expected. His colleague in Houston had called him the devil and, if Sully's not-so-tongue-in-cheek response was to be believed, so had his father. Jessica sensed the darkness in Sully's soul, but she couldn't bring herself to accept that Sully embraced it. There was too much anger in him for there to be much peace. He fought the darkness every step of the way.

She'd seen him pull himself back from the edge. The darkness didn't own him because he used it. His anger was like a shield, something he could focus outward. Jessica envied him that ability. Her anger was always bottled up, a physical thing pressing against her ribs.

"Do you care what people expect?" she asked finally.

When he didn't answer, the silence wove a spell of intimacy around them. The world suddenly narrowed to the two of them, and she didn't like it. Didn't like the way he made every second seem a victory. He was waiting for her to do something stupid—like give in to the impulse inside her that urged her to take one tiny step closer.

A second before she gave in, Jessica broke the spell. "What was Iris talking about, Sully? Who cries for you?"

A slow, sinful smile crossed his face, as if he'd been anticipating the question or her retreat. When he spoke, his tone was patronizing. "Jessie, Jessie, you didn't buy into that sleep-talk, did you? Iris is an adorable flake. Who knows what she was dreaming about at the time."

"Yeah, I bought it," Jessica confessed and pushed past him. "I bought it because you looked like you'd seen a ghost."

Sully hauled her around, keeping her from descending the stairs. "Not a ghost, darlin'. An angel."

Her expression must have been incredulous. His grin got bigger, but his eyes were deadly serious.

"Shocking, isn't it? To find out that even Sullivan Kincaid rates an angel. Yessiree, buddy, Sullivan Kincaid, the devil *himself*, has his own personal angel. That's what they tell me anyway."

"Angel? I don't understand."

"I spent yesterday trying to track down our illusive Madame Evangeline, remember? Which means I spent the day with an assortment of psychics. Most of them see auras and feel vibrations and read those cards. But one of them claims to see angels."

"Lucky for you."

"Yeah. Lucky me. She told me mine was weeping."

Good. She stopped crying.

A chill slithered through Jessica as she remembered that when Iris said those words, she had been looking beyond Sully—over his shoulder. Involuntarily Jessica glanced back toward Iris's room.

"Gives you pause, doesn't it?" asked Sully softly. "Shook me up for a second or two. Maybe you should ask her about your angel."

"I don't have one." Her answer was sure and quick.

"Why? Did yours get tired of crying and fly off to find someone who was worth redeeming?"

If Sully's intent had been to wound, he did a fine job. Because he was right. She wasn't worth redeeming; she'd known that for a long time. Jessica covered the pain of the truth with a joke and started down the stairs. "Silly me. When St. Peter was handing out angels, I thought he said, 'bangles.' I had plenty of bracelets, so I very politely said, 'No thank you, sir.' "

"What a shame," Sully commiserated, but he didn't sound sympathetic. "I have a feeling you could use an angel right about now."

"Now is way too late. I could have used one sixteen years ago." Jessica recognized her mistake before Sully even asked the question.

"What happened sixteen years ago, Jessie?"

The only sign of tension as she answered him was the white-knuckled grip she had on the railing. "Puberty."

When he laughed, she breathed again, was safe again. For a while. Until the next time she forgot that Sully's jovial little conversations were intended to trip her up. He was much too good at uncovering her secrets. Telling herself to be careful around him was redundant, not to mention worthless. She'd known to be careful the first time she met him, and so far "knowing" hadn't made any difference.

She kept stepping into his traps, or was maneuvered skillfully into them. No matter how she got there, the result was the same. Sully had another bit of the puzzle, another tidbit to tickle his suspicions. And she was one step closer to disaster.

Lincoln waited impatiently for them in the living room. Sully gave him a thumbnail sketch—Phil's car had been found, no evidence of foul play, and no details were available. Lincoln was visibly shaken, and his frown deepened, but his response was the same as it had been the night before. Nothing unusual had happened in the last few days with the exception of the unlocked door and Jessica's arrival.

"I'd like to see the office," Sully said.

"Is that smart? I didn't think you were on the case," Jessica reminded him.

"Who said anything about the case? I'm just taking a little tour of the house. The office is part of the house, isn't it, Lincoln?"

"Yeah, but I already locked it," Linc apologized. "It seemed like the thing to do. I had the electronic team in to sweep the house. They cleared it. Nothing was planted; nothing was missing, and that's Phil's private room. So I locked it. It's just a button lock, but I don't have a key."

"Nice work." Sully sighed. "Munro gets his money's worth."

Reluctantly Jessica tightened the noose Sully already seemed to have around her neck and volunteered, "I can let you in."

Sully swung around, brows upraised. In unison, he and Lincoln asked, "You have a key?"

"No." She refused to flinch as the men worked it out in their minds.

Lincoln's mouth dropped open in uncertain surprise, but Sully smacked his forehead with the palm of his hand. "Of course. I don't know why I didn't ask you to pick the lock to begin with. Is there anything you can't do?"

"Getting rid of you has been beyond my talents so far," she murmured sweetly as she went to get her kit. "Lincoln, show him where the office is."

When she joined them, Sully timed her. The lady picked the lock in less than five seconds. Impressive. So the kit wasn't a new toy. It obviously wasn't a toy at all.

The longer he was around Jessica Daniels, the more certain he became that the innocence in her kiss was an illusion. There wasn't an ingenuous bone in her body. The flesh on those bones wasn't particularly innocent either, he decided. She'd taken her boots off upstairs and now her bare legs seemed to go on forever.

He wondered if she'd done it on purpose. Part of him, the lunatic part, hoped she had, that she'd made a conscious decision to attract his attention. Jessie chose that precise moment to turn around and look him squarely in the eye, completely unrepentant for her nefarious skill. With the barest push of her fingertips the door swung open. Their gazes locked. She lifted a brow, waiting for the compliment that he wouldn't give.

"You're in," she said finally, forcing him to move.

"Not yet," he whispered as he passed her, unable to resist that familiar urge to rattle her. "But I'd like to be."

As much as he wanted to, he didn't stop to watch her reaction. Lincoln was already inside the office, talking to him, oblivious to the sensual undercurrent between them.

"We couldn't find anything obvious missing the first time," he said, turning in a circle. "That's why I called in the debugging guys. I thought maybe they'd planted something."

Shooting a quick look back at Jessica, Sully realized she'd kept the missing calendar pages secret from Lincoln. She shrugged and offered no explanation. He was beginning to get used to it; he didn't press until Lincoln left them for one of the security checks he seemed so fond of.

"He didn't know the pages were taken," Sully said, closing the last drawer of uninteresting files. "You flipped the calendar over so no one else would notice."

"And he didn't." She stopped rummaging through the trash can and stood up. "I don't think we're going to find anything."

"What are we looking for?" he inquired politely.

"Phil."

He had to smile as he levered himself up. She was quick on her feet, but he wasn't leaving tonight until he had the answers to a couple of questions. And what they were looking for was one of those questions.

For now he asked, "You really believe someone got here first. Why?"

"Phil's office in Houston was immaculate. This one is disheveled. Somebody searched all right."

"Maybe Carol keeps his office in Houston neat and tidy."

"No." She was firm. "Secretaries usually don't mess with the personal stuff. The middle drawer of his desk in Houston would have done an obsessive-compulsive proud. A place for everything, and everything in its place."

"Except the man himself," Sully quipped, then he dragged the conversation back to the original point. "You didn't tell Lincoln about the calendar."

"There wasn't any reason to tell him. Yesterday I

wasn't certain that the office had been searched. Why upset him?"

"Tell me about Lincoln."

Instead of answering right away, she straightened the blotter on the desk. If Sully didn't know better, he'd have accused the woman of nervousness.

"He seems to care for Iris. He's conscientious. Boy, is he conscientious. He was up most of the night last night." She glanced up from the precisely positioned blotter. "I could hear him checking the house."

"Bet that irritated you."

"Why would that bother me?"

"Weren't you waiting for him to go to sleep so you could use your little kit and search the office by yourself?"

"No, I'm a light sleeper."

"I'll just bet." He considered her for a moment. "Maybe you were checking up on Lincoln. Don't you trust the man?"

"As much as I trust anyone."

"That isn't saying a helluva lot." Sully crossed the room and parked his butt on the edge of the desk, daring her to deny it.

"I guess not." He could have sworn he heard regret in her voice. Then she said, "I'd better check on Iris."

Sully reached for her as she walked by, pulling her into the cage of his thighs. He had to force his gaze away from the buttons on that short scrap of material she called a top. Looking into her eyes wasn't much safer. A man could lose himself in a liquid brown gaze like Jessie's. A man could lose himself and never realize when it happened.

"Is there anyone you do trust?" he asked softly, running his hand down her arm to circle her wrist.

"Not for a long time." She cut her gaze down to her wrist and then back to him.

"Don't you trust me, Jessie?"

"You're the last person I'd trust, Sully."

"You're standing here."

"I'm a fool."

"You may be a lot of things, but fool isn't one of them."

At the moment the word innocent seemed more appropriate than anything. Every time he got physically close to her, the balance of power between them shifted subtly. As long as she had a little distance, she led the dance. As soon as he got close she seemed to forget the steps. The confident "one-up" looks were replaced with wary, wide-eyed uncertainty.

And damned if that didn't make him hot. Women never looked at him like that. Not the ones he got close enough to kiss. Women whose expressions reminded him of Jessie's ran for cover, and yet she didn't. She stood her ground, so close, he had to be careful not to tug her hand even a fraction of an inch. If he did, she'd become intimate with a certain part of his anatomy. Of course, if they stood like this much longer, he wouldn't have to tug her hand. Nature would make the introductions for him.

"Poor Jessie," he said suddenly. "Your body trusts me, even if your brain doesn't."

Painful recognition of that truth flashed in her eyes.

"Is that really so bad?" he asked, and moved her hand up onto his thigh, away from danger. "Let's start with something simple and work up to the scary parts. Tell me how long you've had that white streak in your hair."

He saw the shadow cross her face, and she deflected the question. "Since I met you."

"Funny. Carol said you've had it longer."

She would have pulled away, but he circled her wrist again and caught her elbow. The effect was that she was snug against him now, his thighs rubbing hers.

"You talked with Carol? About me?" she asked in an irritated unhappy-camper voice.

"Uh-huh." He nodded. All the play had gone out of their game, and he was in deadly earnest now. "She said to tell you how sorry she was for not recognizing you immediately, but her mind was just so preoccupied with those government thugs that she wasn't thinking straight."

The anxiety in her eyes evaporated. "Oh, well. It's been a couple of years since I retired."

"Yeah, she said it'd been a couple of years." Sully waited a minute, waited for Jessica to feel safe, and then he added, "She also said that you don't work for Munro Security, and that you never have."

EIGHT

Everything inside Jessica went cold, the way it did whenever the crosshairs of her scope zeroed a target. There had been no room for emotion then, no room for doubt as she followed orders and pulled the trigger. This time, she went cold and motionless because *she* was the target. She was the one in the crosshairs.

Sully had caught her in another trap, and he was playing with her—the way a lazy mountain lion played with a hapless mouse. The instant the lion bored with the creature, the game would be over. Still, the poor stupid mouse kept dodging and darting, pretending it could escape right up to the last minute.

Right until the lion devoured it.

Despite the coolness in Sully's gaze, Jessica knew he was still fascinated with the game. Otherwise, he would have pounced on her the minute he talked to Carol. Pounced and hauled her back to the Houston police. So, the mouse was alive for a while, but it was time to dazzle him. Time to let him draw a little blood. Time to boost his interest in the chase.

Slowly, enunciating each word carefully, she told

him, "I don't recall ever saying that I worked for Munro Security."

"Don't split hairs with me. I'm not in the mood." His hand tightened painfully on her elbow. "I was there when Iris said you were one of Phil's top people. You didn't deny it."

Refusing to grimace, Jessica said, "Obviously, you didn't listen to Iris. I worked for *Phil*. Not Munro Security. I doubt Carol, or anyone at Munro Security for that matter, knows about Phil's dirty little dozen."

She could see the wheels turning in Sully's head. He was a smart guy. He'd add two and two real quick. Now all she could do was hope his sum was something other than four. He looked away and then back at her as the tumblers of his mind clicked into place.

"Carol might not know about the dirty dozen, but I bet the CIA does. Am I right?"

She nodded and thought he'd be pleased with himself for figuring it out, but he frowned instead.

"That's what this is all about, isn't it? Some secret little group of professionals Munro put together to handle special jobs for the government, right?"

He pushed her away suddenly as if he needed space to breathe. He paced the room, shaking his head the whole time. Jessica rubbed her arm and let him come to his own conclusions. Finally he whipped around as if he couldn't deny the obvious any longer.

"You're a spy."

"I didn't say that." Jessica protested a little too quickly, but salved her conscience with the knowledge that she was telling the truth. If Sully jumped to conclusions based on her tone and timing, it was his own fault.

He laughed in disbelief. "Of course not. No one

admits they're a spook. That's what they teach you, isn't it? How to lie convincingly? You're pretty good."

It wasn't a compliment.

Crossing her arms over her midriff, she waited him out, neither denying or confirming anything. At this point his creativity was working in her favor. Good cops were always able to piece a story together from thin air. The trick was in making him use more air than fact.

"What's your specialty?" he asked in the same tone people used at cocktail parties to ask someone's line of work. "I would imagine it's getting inside places you have no business being inside. You were awfully fast with that lock for someone who's been retired two years. You must practice."

"Any idiot can order a lock-pick kit out of a number of magazines. That doesn't make them spies."

His eyes ran over her, appraising her. "What is the job description for a spy nowadays? I bet you did a lot more than pick locks for the government."

"Does any of that really matter now?" The irritation in her voice was real. She didn't want him traveling any farther down this path. "I haven't worked for Phil or anyone else in two *years*. I'm involved in this mess only because a scared little girl called me. Don't you get it, Sully? I'm floundering around just like you. I don't know anything."

The coldness inside her was gone, replaced with the warm buzz of blossoming anger. Without realizing it, she had taken a step toward him with each sentence until the mouse was once again within reach of the mountain lion. Pride wouldn't let her retreat. Not this time. The man affected her on so many levels, she'd lost count.

All she knew for sure was that if she let him pick

the battles between them, she'd lose the war. Jessica wasn't certain what was at stake, but she'd rather go down in flames than fly a white flag or run for the hill country. Jessica Daniels had never given up or run from anything since she was thirteen years old, and even then she'd settled the score first.

So why was Sully different from the others? Why did he unsettle her and trigger her fight or flight instincts? Why couldn't she just ignore him instead of baiting him?

For some obscure reason, Jessica didn't want Sully to think her a coward. Whatever happened would just have to happen. She wasn't going to avoid the current flowing between them anymore or pretend it wasn't there. Ignoring it only made it worse.

"I'm not the bad guy here," Jessica said quietly.

"If you're not the bad guy . . . then who is?" he asked, taking a step of his own, decreasing the distance between them. All that remained now was a scant inch. His eyes bored into hers as he looked down. "If you don't know anything, then what the hell are you looking for, Jessie?"

"The same thing everyone else is," she quipped. "A good night's sleep and another chance to do it right." Then she ruined the flip answer when she added a melancholy footnote. It was a reflex really. "Neither of which are possible."

"Why not?" His question was unexpectedly full of gentleness.

"Because no one gets a second chance. You can't go back and do your life over. Even if you want to."

Sully knew the truth when he heard it. Or maybe he knew this truth in particular because it hit so close to home. Although . . . if he could, even if he wanted to, he wouldn't go back and change a thing. He'd stopped lying to himself years ago. What was done, was done. Written on his soul in indelible ink.

"What would you change, Jessie?" he asked, the need to get inside her head getting the better of him as it always did. The other questions, the cop questions, could wait until she wasn't close enough to kiss, until the faint scent of flowers in the summer rain didn't drift over his mind like a mist.

Right now all he cared about was the woman. And the woman wasn't backing away for once.

"Tell me," he urged. "What would you change?"

"Simple." Her crooked half smile squeezed his heart as she said, "I'd change me."

He reached out to trace the line of her arm, from elbow to shoulder. This close to Jessie he always wanted to touch her. "Oh no, you're wrong about that. Changing Jessica Daniels would be a mistake."

She took a deep breath. "I'm good at mistakes."

"Name one."

Suddenly their positions seemed so intimate to Jessica. They were no longer adversaries squaring off; they were like lovers maneuvering for position. She swallowed, dropped her gaze to his mouth, and named the first mistake she could think of. "Kissing you. That was a big mistake."

"I don't think so." He smoothed his hand slowly along her shoulder to the side of her neck. "The mistake is taking all the blame for yourself. Shouldn't you be making excuses? Telling me the devil made you do it? Protesting your virtue? Spouting indignant declarations that it won't happen again?" His face was so close to hers. "Most women would."

Her breathing was noticeably shallow, but her voice held steady as his thumb rubbed the side of her throat. "Not me. I don't make promises I can't keep. Not anymore."

Sully eased his hand to the back of her neck, letting his fingers spear through her hair until he could massage her through the curtain of silk. "So, you're a woman of her word. That's pretty ironic coming from you, don't you think?"

His words would have rankled Jessica if his fingers hadn't been performing a dangerous magic on her muscles and bones. Or if his voice hadn't been a raspy whisper that swirled heat in the most unlikely places. She had to divide her attention between focusing on the conversation and making her legs support her.

She defended herself and her integrity with a simple alibi because it was all she could manage. "I never made you a promise, so I couldn't have broken one."

"I'll keep that in mind."

He tilted her head and pulled her to him. Jessica knew what was coming, but having been kissed by him before didn't prepare her for this. Sully's mouth was hot and sure. He cradled her head with both hands as his tongue swept through the barrier of her lips without the tender forays of the morning.

This kiss was unfinished business. It stripped her of her common sense before his hands ever left her head. She was open to him, and he knew it. Surrender was the only way to describe how she felt. Like she'd given herself up to the wicked pulse that began to throb inside her as the heat of his mouth fanned the flame of an unfamiliar warmth between her legs. Of their own accord, her arms snaked around his neck so she could press the length of her body against him without anything in the way except their clothing.

When Jessie softened, Sully's arousal jumped in response. Just like this morning there was something about Jessie that got inside him and made him forget the rest of the world, forget his responsibilities. Made him even forget the darkness.

He couldn't think past the feel of her against him or the need to explore what she offered. Kissing her was like sinking into light. He slid his hand down over her collarbone, over the swell of her breast until her nipple rested in the hollow of his palm. He smiled against her mouth as she pushed into his hand, silently asking for more.

Obliging, Sully trailed his mouth downward, flicking his tongue against the base of her throat as his fingers grated across her pebbled nipple. A ragged sigh rewarded him. Now he was the one who wanted more —more sounds from Jessie. Capturing her mouth again, he cupped her rump with his hands, his fingertips almost beyond the edge of her skirt.

He rolled his hips against hers, settling his hardness against softness. Once. Twice. And then she moaned for him. Just a half sound in the back of her throat, the kind of sound a woman made when desire rocked her unexpectedly.

The denim was soft and pliable in his hands, easily gathered up, but he didn't gather it. Not yet. Instead he let his hand wander over one gently rounded hip, toward the center of her belly, and then beneath the skirt. Jessie tensed as he pulled the material up. He could feel her backing away by the microsecond.

"Let me," he whispered against her mouth. "Trust me."

She caught her breath and held herself still, as if moving would shatter her somehow. She wasn't the only one ready to shatter. Sully was rock-hard, and the hell of it was they were both fully clothed.

Taking his time, Sully let her adjust to the feel of

his hand against her bare skin. He toyed with the edge of her underwear, tucking his index finger inside and rubbing from side to side. All the while keeping her mouth busy. Finally he splayed his hand flat against her abdomen, fingers down, inside her panties.

Crisp curls—he didn't even know the color, he realized—teased the pads of his fingers. But he didn't shift downward, didn't touch her. Not until Jessie raised up on her toes, just a bit, just enough to let him know she wanted him to keep going.

Sully figured that admission of need had cost her a lot. Even so, he held back for a second, letting his mouth find her shoulder, pulling her bra strap and shirt aside as he dropped kisses on the bare skin. When her fingers dug into his shoulders, clutching handfuls of his shirt, he touched her finally.

Her sharp, desperate intake of breath was everything he could have hoped for. The next sharp breath was his own as his finger slid into her. Jessie was hot, and wet, and tight.

Need rolled through him like a train at midnight. He wanted to take her. Just rip her panties away and sink himself to the hilt. No bed, just here. Right now. While she was wet. Before Jessie remembered she didn't trust him. Before he remembered that he didn't trust her. Before the world interrupted them.

The phone rang, and Sully cursed. It already was too late. Jessie was surfacing for air. She froze in his arms as the phone rang a second time. Reluctantly he removed his hand, but he made damn sure she felt every second of his retreat, forcing a gasp from her as he flicked the sensitive nub. The blush on her face as she straightened her skirt would have done a virgin proud.

"Been a while, Jessie?" he asked, irritated at her

ability to make him feel as though he'd been the villain instead of a partner in crime. And he was fairly certain what they did to each other physically was a crime. No one else had ever been able to make him react so quickly.

Before she could answer, the phone rang a third time.

"Where's Lincoln?" Sully growled. "Isn't answering the phone his job?"

"He's probably outside." Her voice was shaky, and she refused to look at him. "He checks all the gates, all the windows, and every door."

"Busy fellow."

Ring.

"Aren't you all?" Jessica mumbled as she gave up and went to the phone. She grabbed it on the next ring, afraid it would wake Iris, and relieved to have something to do that didn't require looking at Sully. She was still shaking from their encounter. Her palms were sweaty, and her lungs needed more oxygen than she could quietly suck in.

"Munro residence."

She heard silence, not the kind of silence from a dead connection, but the breathy silence of someone waiting on the other end. Her heart thudded heavily against her rib cage as she realized the first move was up to her.

"I'm sorry," she said into the void, trying to sound as normal as possible, as if she were answering a request for Phil to come to the phone. She was playing a dangerous game, trying to convince whoever was on the line to talk while convincing Sully that it was a routine call. "Phil isn't here at the moment. I'm Jessica Daniels. I could take a message if it's important."

"We have him. Is that important?"

"I see."

"We'd rather have the book."

Jessica fought the clenching of her jaw and the urge to turn away from Sully. Instead she rolled her eyes and held the phone a little way from her ear as if she'd been yelled at. "You might try later. I know you're in a bind but that's about the only advice I can give you at the moment."

"Police?"

"Yes, that's right." The phone clicked, but Jessica didn't hang up. Her heart was still in her throat as she said, "You could try his secretary tomorrow. She might have his updated schedule. Uh-huh. Bye, now."

Slowly she lowered the receiver and met Sully's gaze. He narrowed his eyes, on the verge of suspicion. She had about three seconds to nip it in the bud. "It was some sort of computer security foul-up at Texacon. The jerk wouldn't leave a message, and I felt weird saying that Phil's unaccounted for."

"That was Texacon?" he queried skeptically, walking toward her. "On Phil's beach house line?"

Jessica threw up her hands and enacted a drama. "You caught me, Detective. It was really Phil's kidnappers. They're going to call me back tonight as soon as I get rid of you and I can talk. Of course that could get sticky unless I get to the phone before Lincoln." She put her hands on her hips as she finished and nailed him with a glare intended to make him sorry he ever doubted her. "Who the hell do you think it was?"

"When you put it like that, I guess it was Texacon."

"Smart guess."

Relief flooded through her as the outrageous confession soothed Sully's misgivings; his frown eased and his brow unfurrowed. One hurdle passed. Now all she had to do was get rid of him.

That wasn't going to be easy, not without triggering his suspicions all over again. She didn't need him involved. He couldn't help anyway; he didn't know where the book was. And he couldn't possibly know these people the way she did. She didn't want to think about what they might have already done to Phil.

No, she had to handle it her way. All Sully could do was make her regret her choices and want what she couldn't have.

At the moment that wasn't a hard feat to pull off. Not when he stood there with starburst wrinkles in the material of his shirt, wrinkles she'd put there by grabbing hold of him to steady herself. The last few seconds in his arms blazed through her mind, crowding out rational thought. Even now she could feel his hands on her, stroking, entering her. The horrible reality was that spending time with Sullivan Kincaid was dangerous, and she wanted more anyway. She wanted what would have happened if the phone hadn't rung.

Right man, wrong place. Wrong time. Wrong world. Jessica Daniels had killed people; Sullivan Kincaid was a cop. That was a match made in hell. A chasm much too wide to cross. At least in this lifetime.

Sully watched the regret seep into Jessie's expression. Second thoughts were a nasty way to spend time, and she was having a few. Maybe more than a few considering what happened between them. His only regret was that the phone rang too soon.

"Say it," he ordered.

"Say what?"

"How we've just made another mistake."

"Surely you could figure that out for yourself?"

"I'm funny that way. I like things spelled out."

"It was a mistake. G-o A-W-A-Y."

"No such luck. At least not until we settle a few things."

"Everything's settled. The Houston police are looking for Phil. Iris is safe and sound in her bed. Texacon is going to make Carol's life miserable instead of mine. Lincoln is here to protect us. What else is there to settle?"

"Why you fall apart in my arms, and how I could get used to it with very little encouragement."

"It's your imagination."

"Not this time."

"Nothing happened. We kissed. I—we got a little carried away. Subject closed."

"Yeah, you already told me how you get a little carried away sometimes. If that's how you react to a kiss, then lead me to the bedroom, darlin', 'cause I can't wait to see what happens during foreplay."

"That's not ever going to happen."

"Sounds like a promise."

"It is."

"Are you sure you can keep this one?"

Jessica wondered how he did it. How he found the secret buttons and pushed them. She wasn't certain at all, but she'd never admit it. "Go away, Sully."

"I will. Just as soon as you tell me what you and the CIA are looking for. And why it's so important that you find it."

NINE

Jessica ground the heels of her hands into her temples and then raked her fingers through her hair. For the first time Sully noticed the shadows beneath her eyes. She really hadn't slept the night before, and he found himself curbing the temptation to pull her toward him and lay her head on his chest.

The impulse blew him away. Over the years he'd been involved with a number of women, but he could honestly say that comfort had never been a part of the package. *I don't trust you as far as I can throw you, Jessie girl, and yet I worry about you. Ain't that a helluva note.*

With a resigned sigh, she began to talk. "I think it was the CIA who searched here. I can't swear to it, but it's a reasonable assumption if Iris called them from Phil's phone. They'd be anxious."

"About what?"

"Phil's little black book of personnel."

"His team of spies? Wouldn't they already have that information?"

"No." Jessica rubbed her temples again, this time with her fingers. "No one but Phil has it. He swore to me that he kept our names in a little black book that was as safe as Fort Knox. Other than that there weren't supposed to be files on us. Nothing to tie us to Phil. Nothing to tie us to the government. The name of the game was deniability. We all knew that going in. The payments were even transferred from one Swiss bank account to another."

"So how did Iris find you?"

"She went by the Houston office last week to say good-bye to her dad before coming down here. That's where she saw the file with my name and phone number. The folder was lying open on his desk."

"Well, wasn't that convenient."

Glaring at him, she continued, "It makes a weird kind of sense. He was always trying to get me back for one more job. If he lied to me about having files, then she could have seen mine on his desk. My number's an easy one to remember. The last four digits are all the same."

"Okay, I'll buy it."

Jessica gritted her teeth. "I wasn't selling anything." She turned and walked out into the entertainment room. "Lock up on your way out, Detective."

"Why bother?" he called. "The only one this lock seems to keep out is Iris."

In spite of herself, Jessica felt the tug at the corners of her mouth. He had a point. Nevertheless she heard the click of the lock as he pushed it in and the thud of the solid wood doors as he closed them.

For good measure, Sully rattled the doorknobs and then followed her. He could have lengthened his stride and caught her, but he decided he liked the view. With legs like that, the lady was made for sin. There was something incredibly sexy about her walk and the soft, intimate sound of bare feet on wood flooring. Even from behind he could tell that Jessie had her arms wrapped around her stomach—as if she was holding herself together.

Holding her temper together was more like it, he decided. He admired a woman who didn't fall to pieces. He imagined it would take a lot to shake Jessie. Kisses seemed to do the trick, but not much else so far.

"I understand why the CIA is looking for that book, but why are you looking so hard for it?" he asked her very straight back. She didn't break stride, but he saw her fingers curl into fists.

"That's pretty obvious. National security and all that. I'm as patriotic as the next person."

"A desperate patriot maybe. You skipped the file cabinets completely tonight, but you looked under the rug, behind the pictures on the wall, at the bottom of his desk drawers. You even looked in the trash can, darlin'. You were *desperately* hoping they left it behind."

"Who the hell are you? Columbo?" Jessica whirled on him—arms akimbo—at the opening into the foyer, trapping him in the hallway. "Can't you ever follow any kind of questioning pattern? If you want to know something, just ask me instead of ambushing me over and over. I'm tired of the games. So why don't you ask all of your questions—questions that you're not *even* supposed to be asking because you aren't on the case— and then get out."

Sully kept right on walking toward her as she talked. It was a pedestrian version of chicken. To her credit she didn't move until he put his hands on her shoulders and moved her.

"Is there a problem?" Lincoln asked from a little above them as he came slowly down the stairs.

"The detective was just leaving," Jessica said as Sully dropped his hands.

"I'll walk him out."

"No," she corrected Lincoln firmly. "I'll do it."

"You sure? I'd be happy to help."

Surprised to find that Lincoln wasn't overly fond of Sully either, Jessica nodded. For one thing she wanted her gun back, and for another she wanted the questions over with. "Yeah. I'm sure. I'll do it."

"Well, if we're all through banding together against the policeman," Sully commented sarcastically, "why don't you show me out, Jessie?"

No one said a word as they crossed the marble foyer and slipped out the door. The contrast of the cool polished stone and the rough brick paving beneath her feet reminded her of dealing with Sully. Things went along so smoothly and then hit a rough patch.

This was probably going to be another rough patch.

Sully didn't move toward his car. His hands were in his front pockets as he gazed out over the lawn. "How much does Lincoln know?"

"Nothing but what Iris told him. I'm a friend of the family he hadn't had the opportunity to meet. The way she treats me pretty much supports that story. Next question."

"I saw your face when you realized the suits had beat you to Phil's company office. Why the fear? You work for them. So what if your name's in the book?"

Jessica took a long time to answer. This question was simply another method of figuring out why she wanted the book so badly. He'd just keep asking it, a hundred different ways until he tripped her up, so she cut the misery short.

"I want the book, because I'm retired, and I'd rather not be reactivated. If they don't have the book, they can't ask."

He turned finally and looked at her. "Just say no."

"You ever tried saying no to the government?"

"Can't say that I have."

First Jessica swirled her hair into a knot and let it hang down her back, out of her way. Then she took a deep breath. "They're really good at making it impossible to say no. I don't want them to have another shot at me. You understand? I walked away once already."

"And no one's ever done that?"

"From Phil's team?" She laughed bitterly. "No. I imagine the powers-that-be had stress heart attacks when he told them an operative took a hike. That's one of the reasons I'm here now. I owe him enough to help his little girl."

Jessica walked onto the lawn, her feet sinking into the thick, supple grass that would have cost a fortune to keep green in the Texas heat if not for the Gulf rains. She wiggled her toes and wished she had pockets in her skirt. She wanted someplace to put her hands because she was afraid they might shake. Afraid if Sully got too close, she might reach for him.

"Why'd he let you go?" Sully asked. He didn't follow her onto the lawn, instead he stood back and let her have some space. When she faced him, her eyes were shiny. Too shiny.

"Let it drop, Sully. It doesn't have anything to do with his disappearance. I promise, okay? Next question."

"You want the book. They want the book. Who else wants it?"

"I imagine anyone who knows Phil is missing. Whoever finds the book or the files will control the team. Our codes are in the book. Take your pick. Any job. Anywhere. Anytime. Most of them don't care what they do as long as you have the code."

"Codes? Are you serious?"

"As death and taxes," she told him flatly. "That's how it works. You get a phone call. Phil gives you the code. You get a package of information. You do the job. You call him afterward, give him the code and the status. I don't imagine anyone would kick if it wasn't Phil's voice. Not if the voice had the code. Next question."

Sully dragged a nagging thought forward. "Isn't it a tad foolish to keep a book like this?"

"How many phone numbers can you memorize?" She interrupted as he opened his mouth to answer, and added, "When people move a lot. When people get killed and have to be replaced. And unless someone knows what the information is, what are they going to do with the book anyway? Everybody carries day planners, pocket calendars, electronic organizers. It wouldn't even look odd. Besides that, Phil was surrounded by security!"

"Someone got in to search the office."

"You think I don't know that?" Jessica asked unhappily, walking back to the pavement.

"Who do you think has it?"

"I don't know. It could still be on Phil," Jessica lied. "Or some mugger could have thrown it in the trash. If that's true then we're all spinning our wheels for nothing. Next question, and speed it up. I really do need to check on Iris."

Sully looked up at the moon, his hands on his hips. "I'm not sure I have a next question. All I know is that Harlan is going to love this Hollywood plot." He shook his head. "Goldilocks, a missing millionaire, a code book, the CIA, and Mata Hari. It's a helluva a fairy tale."

"Are you planning to read Harlan this bedtime story?"

"Not on your life." He shot a glance at her and started for his car. "I've had all the butt chewing I can stand for a day or two."

"What are you going to do?"

"I'm going to give Peter a call at home and see if our friends, the suits, visited them today." Sully yanked open his door and folded his long frame behind the wheel. "If the suits have taken over the investigation, then they already know everything we know. There's nothing to do."

Jessica shut the door, and when the electric window slid down she asked, "And if they haven't taken over?"

"I don't know, Jessie." Sully reached for something in the glove compartment and then handed her the derringer. He looked at her hard as he started the engine. "I don't know."

Iris's room looked different at night. All the rainbow colors disappeared into shades of gray, the purples into black. There wasn't even a night-light, but Jessica wasn't surprised. Iris wasn't the kind of kid who'd need a night-light.

Staring down at her, Jessica lost track of time. She wondered how often Iris's friends slept over, filling up that empty twin bed. She wondered a lot of things as she stood there. There was something so peaceful about Iris's face. And finally it was that peacefulness that had Jessica wondering if she'd made the right choice that night. She was playing God with this child's father. Maybe she should have told Sully about the call, trusted the police or the FBI to find Phil before they killed him.

No, she told herself, refusing to second-guess a decision that was already made. She and Iris didn't need a bunch of tin heroes looking to make promotion. They needed that book. Iris said she'd never seen a book like that.

It wasn't downstairs. The suits had dragged off a mountain of files to go through, so she had to assume they hadn't found anything obvious in Phil's office. Yet. But she seriously doubted they were worried about Phil's life. The way they played the game it was every man for himself. If they couldn't find the book, the agency might, just might, begin to worry about getting Phil back alive.

Jessica grasped the corners of the spread and pulled it over Iris, who lay scrunched up in the fetal position with her hands curled under her chin. Covering her up should have been simple, but it wasn't simple at all. Tucking a child in was like making a promise—a promise that you'd be there when they woke. A promise to watch over them while they slept.

Such a big promise, Jessica thought. One that was made every day by millions of people. She wondered if it still felt so important after you'd done it hundreds and hundreds of times.

Pausing, she tried to remember if she'd ever been tucked in, and she couldn't. She remembered a cavalcade of nannies turning off the lights, and she remembered lying in bed whispering to Jenny. They'd always shared a room, even though there were plenty of bedrooms in her father's house. They'd had twin beds, and nannies who hated trying to keep them from talking all night. An unexpected grin grabbed hold of her as she recalled how many times they'd had to bury their faces in pillows to muffle the laughter. A snort always managed to leak out somehow and bring whatever dragon had been hired to watch them that week.

They hadn't had a night-light either. Didn't need one. They had each other. The smile faded as Jessica realized exactly when she'd begun to hate the dark. Glancing over at the empty twin bed, she ordered herself not to cry. Her chin crumpled anyway. It always had a mind of its own.

And once the tears arrived so did the impossible wish. Jessica stared at that bed and wished as hard as she'd ever wished in her life, and when she was through, she was still alone. Jenny was still dead. And she couldn't forgive herself for being alive. Or for what she had become. Wishing never changed a thing, but she always tried.

"If wishes were wings," she whispered to the empty bed, in a barely audible voice, "then frogs wouldn't bump their butts when they hopped."

Jenny thought that was about the funniest thing their father had ever said to them, and he had come up with some beauts. Never appropriate to the occasion, never remotely wise, but well worth repeating late at night after the lights went out. Uncertainly Jessica touched an index finger to one lock of Iris's hair.

"Sleep tight," Jessica breathed and turned away. She'd had about all the pain she could take for one night.

"Jessie?"

It was such a tiny word, and it cut her heart open. For a split second, time flew backward, sucking her into a memory she didn't want and couldn't stop.

—◆—————————◆—

"Jessie?"

"What?"

"I don't like it," Jenny whispered. "It's too dark."

They huddled beside each other on the bed, which was a dirty mattress thrown on a rusty old frame. Jessie, the older twin by three minutes and twenty-nine seconds, leaned back against the wall and made it unanimous. "I hate the dark."

Jenny leaned back, too, pulling her arms inside her favorite T-shirt for warmth. It read—I SHOT J. R. GIVE ME THE MEDAL. "It's getting colder. Do you think they're going to starve us?"

"No. Daddy won't pay them if they hurt us. I think starving counts as hurting us, so they can't do that. At least I don't think so. Why would they? All they want is the money. That's what they said. Just the money."

"Just a couple of days."

Unspoken between them was the fear that their abductors had lied. Silence, which had never bothered them before, was suddenly like a third person in the room, a threat to be wiped out.

"Jessie?"

"What?"

"I hope Daddy pays them soon."

"Me too."

"Jessie?"

"What?"

"Is it going to be okay?"

"Yeah. I promise."

"Jessie?" Iris called again, raising her voice as she sat up. "Are you okay? Is it my dad?"

"No!" But she didn't turn around.

That's when Iris knew she'd been crying. Adults hated to let anyone see them cry, so Iris stayed put and took a couple of deep breaths with her hand on her harmony ball. The sinking feeling in the pit of her stomach wasn't any worse, so nothing else could have happened to her dad.

"I didn't mean to wake you, kiddo," Jessica said as she wiped the moisture away from her eyes and swung around.

"That's okay. I don't like being alone."

"Me either."

"You can sleep in here tonight."

Smiling at the way Iris so easily offered comfort, Jessica said, "Maybe I will."

"You would really?"

"Sure." Jessica sat on the bed, crooking one leg beneath her and letting the other rest on the floor. This close she could see Iris well enough to read her expression. "How are you holding up?"

Iris reached for her hand, which Jessica gave to her without hesitation this time. She knew the drill. After a minute, Iris let go and said, "Better than you."

The ghost of a smile crossed Jessica's face. "You got me at a bad time. I've just spent the better part of the evening being grilled by our favorite detective. That'd ruin just about anyone's aura."

"I like him." Iris fluffed her pillows up behind her and leaned back. "Why does he make you sad?"

"He doesn't. The man makes me nuts!"

"So who makes you sad?"

"Who says I'm sad?"

Iris pressed her lips together in a letter-perfect imitation of an old maid schoolteacher who's just been lied to. "Well, you were crying, and when I hold your hand you make me want to cry. What would you call it?"

"Okay. So I'm a little sad," Jessica confessed. "I miss my sister sometimes. She died when she was barely older than you."

"I'm sorry."

"It's okay. That was a long time ago. You remind me of her sometimes. Like when you called me Jessie. She called me that too."

"So does Sully."

"Yeah, I noticed," Jessica complained wryly.

"You want us to stop?"

Amazed, Jessica realized she really didn't. "No. You keep right on. It's kind of nice now that I'm used to it again."

"Good." Iris nodded her head as though new Middle East peace accords had been signed. "Because you aren't a Jessica."

That forced a laugh. "Thank you. I think. That's what your dad always said to me—that I wasn't a Jessica. I guess you and he are a lot alike."

Clasping her hands on her lap, Iris asked, "Did he ever say anything about me?"

"Of course," Jessica lied. "He talked about you all the time. How proud he was of you. How smart you were. How pretty."

"He really thinks I'm pretty?"

"No. He thinks you're gorgeous and that he's going to have to hire fifteen more Lincolns to keep the boys away."

"Do you think he's coming back?"

The quiet question came at Jessica out of nowhere, and she didn't know how to answer it. How could she answer it? Once more she had the feeling that she was *the* grown-up in a child's world. That position magically bestowed her with the intuition of the universe as far as Iris was concerned.

Yet the only intuition Jessica possessed, she didn't intend to share with a child. She believed that Phil's time on earth was currently numbered in hours. As long as the book was missing, he stayed alive, but it was only a matter of time before someone found it. Then Phil became expendable, depending on the point of view of whoever had the book.

Once the kidnappers had the book, they wouldn't want Phil around to screw up their plans. They'd kill him. Even if he made it to the exchange site alive, Phil was dead the moment the book changed hands. And if by some twist of fate the book was never found, Phil would be just as dead because he'd be excess baggage to the kidnappers.

Instead of saying any of that, Jessica asked her own question. "If we had a way to get your dad back, would you want to take it?"

Iris leaned forward. "Yes."

"Even if it meant not telling the police?"

"Like ransom? Like if he's been kidnapped?"

"Yeah. Exactly like that."

"Couldn't we tell Sully?"

"Especially not Sully."

"Why not?"

"Because this isn't about punishing the bad guys or getting evidence. This is about getting your dad back, and I don't think I can do it if my hands are tied by the police. I don't want to have to follow their rules."

Iris watched her without expression. "Sully would make you do that?"

"He wouldn't have a choice." *He has to play fair. He*

*can't kill the bad guys before the exchange to save your
father.*

"What happens if we do it your way?" Iris asked.

"We wait for a call. We offer them whatever they
want. And I pick the time and place for the exchange
to make sure they bring your daddy."

"And if we told Sully?"

The bad guys won't be dead when we're done.

"Sort of the same thing. Except I wouldn't be there
at the exchange."

"Oh, no!" Iris said quickly. She scrambled up on
her knees, leaning forward. Right before she grabbed
Jessica's arm, she stopped herself and clasped her
hands on her thighs. "You have to be there. I don't
know why, but you have to. I knew you were the one
as soon as you answered the phone."

"No," Jessica got up, rubbing away the chill bumps
on her arms. Only one other person in her life had had
this kind of blind faith in her, and Jenny was dead
because of it. "No, don't think like that. I'm not here
because of some cosmic plan. I'm here because I was
the only phone number you could remember."

But Iris kept looking at her with that eerie certainty, making Jessica wonder what she'd done to deserve such trust. *Besides giving orders and sweeping in
here like you had all the answers? Like you were the hero of
an action-adventure film come to save the day? You wanted
the job, and now you've got it.*

"I don't come with a guarantee, Iris. All I can do is
what I can do, and it may not be enough."

"It will be." Iris slipped down off the bed. "I've got
to brush my teeth and wash my face." With that she
was gone, subject closed, life-altering decision made.

Jessica was left alone in the dark with the conse-
quences of her arrogance, fighting the dread and nau-

sea that threatened. The first thing she did was flip on the light to dispel the shadows, but the cheerful colors didn't have time to work their magic. The shrill jangle of the phone shattered the silence even before her hand dropped away from the switch plate.

TEN

Welcome to Jericho. Life's a beach.

Sully pulled back the screen door and unlocked the faded wood one to let himself in. His beach house was a far cry from the Munro estate, and only supposed to be temporary. Casa Kincaid—in the less affluent section of the island where the houses were mostly rented by the week to middle-class tourists—had weathered a number of violent storms and had the scars to prove it. However, the house suited Sully, who'd also weathered a number of violent storms and had the scars to prove it.

On stilts and wrapped by a porch, the place had become home so quickly that Sully couldn't imagine living anywhere else. Or maybe it was the solitude of the beach at night. He dragged a hand through his hair and tossed his keys on the scuffed coffee table that had come with the house. The gun, his tie, and his wallet followed as he melted into heaven. Heaven was an easy chair that he'd spent the better part of five years training to fit every nook, cranny, and bone of Sullivan

Kincaid to a T. Tonight, he sorely needed that chair to ease his sorrows.

Jessie Daniels was hard on a man.

His mouth twisted into an unwilling smile. No argument there.

Jessie had the art of man-frustration down to a science. Without visible effort on her part, she had all of his senses wrapped up in three separate and incredibly complicated issues—the lady, the case, and her body. Sully closed his eyes and decided a woman shouldn't be able to lie with a mouth that could kiss like that. One accomplishment was a talent and the other a sin. Hell of it was, he just couldn't figure out which was which.

And he needed to figure it out. Quick.

As far as he could tell, Jessie was dangerous for someone like himself, someone who'd sworn to keep his life simple. She stirred things inside him that other women had never been able to touch. When he looked at her, emotions shifted in his chest and common sense disappeared. Jessie was dangerous all right, because she wasn't the kind of woman a man could walk away from.

The image of her on the driveway as he drove out the gate stuck in his mind. Barefoot and hugging herself, she didn't look capable of taking care of *Jessie*, much less Iris. But he knew better. He knew there was steel beneath the softness. The woman was a chameleon. That was the only reason he hadn't turned the car around.

Well, if he were completely honest, the gate closing had something to do with it.

Perspective was a lovely thing, Sully admitted. He could use a little more of it in handling Jessie. *Handling*

Jessie. Now there was an idea with merit. Sully smiled again and regretfully hauled himself out of the chair.

He had work to do. He couldn't sit there all night spinning fantasies while the real world waited. Cop instinct took precedence over base instinct. Jessie was damn close to changing that, though. He definitely needed perspective.

The phone was in the kitchen, which meant he could at least grab a beer before calling Peter Keelyn. Inexplicably Sully felt the need to fortify himself when it came to dealing with Jessie in any way, shape, or form. As he walked past the answering machine, he pushed the flashing message button and pulled his shirttail from his jeans.

The beer hadn't even made it out of the refrigerator before Sully set it back down and closed the door. He leaned against the cold metal surface and stared at the answering machine.

"Hey, this is Peter. You know that feeling you had? Guess what? The freakin' *CI of A* crashed the Munro party this afternoon. They shut down everything, flashed a ton of ID, and every third word was 'national security.' They asked for full cooperation on this one. Then told us to go twiddle our thumbs until further notice. Nobody's to breathe a word or make a move without clearing it. No media. And Harlan says they've got the juice to make it stick. So watch your back, buddy. They'll be coming your way. Hell, they're probably already there, and you just don't know it. Sneaky bastards."

Sully listened as the machine beeped and whirred and clicked before it finally stopped, leaving the room silent. It was over then. Done. He was out of the loop, and no longer responsible for passing along what he knew.

So where was the closure? Why did the message start that tingle at the base of his spine? Why'd he still feel the need to do something?

Unsettled, Sully hit the message button again. Closing his eyes, he focused on Peter's voice. The man's nose was out of joint, but it was more than that. Peter didn't *trust* them.

". . . they're probably already there, and you just don't know it."

Sully checked his watch. "Aw, hell, when you're right, Peter, you are right."

As the details meshed into a nasty little scenario, Sully grabbed the phone and called the department for confirmation. No . . . they hadn't heard a word from anyone on the Munro case—other than Harlan who indicated it was Houston's baby. Of course you haven't been contacted, Sully thought. The agency wasn't going to be making an official visit to Jericho or Munro's house because they'd already searched the most obvious spot. They weren't worried about recording equipment for ransom calls or alerting the local PD for backup or interviewing witnesses. Or even protecting national security. All they wanted was the book—the last loose thread.

They didn't care how they got it, didn't care if Phil came out of this alive, or even if Jessie and Iris were caught in the crossfire. They were setting Jessie up, waiting to see who else came to the party before they made a move.

After asking for Munro's private number, Sully hung up. What more was there to say that would sound remotely credible? He had nothing but conjecture and hunch to go on. Not a single concrete fact beyond Phil's disappearance and the CIA's appropriation of the investigation. Everything else had come from Jessie. Most of that either lies, half-truths, or grudging admissions to be sifted through carefully.

So why did he believe her?

Because she had nothing to gain.

The agency, on the other hand, had a great deal at stake, and they were willing to sacrifice a couple of innocents if it would lead them to what they wanted. Sully wondered if they wanted the operatives back on-line or if they just wanted them dead.

They'd probably read the Houston incident reports by now. She'd found the calendar and the car, which they'd sloppily missed. Maybe she could find the book for them. Jessie was their tool. Who cared if she ended up dead in the process?

He cared, Sully discovered suddenly. He cared more than he wanted to admit, even to himself. Sparring with Jessie, kissing her, touching her—all of it—pulled him out of himself. Sully wasn't used to that. Nor was he particularly happy. He'd never had anything feel so right and so wrong at the same time.

He dialed the estate and willed it to ring.

Swearing, Sully slammed the phone down. The line was busy. At ten-thirty? Why would they be on the phone at this time of night? He stared at the phone. "You've got five minutes, Jessie. Five."

Jessica spun, searching for the source of the ringing. She found the phone—sitting on the nightstand, half-hidden by the trolls she had moved off the bed earlier. Jessica's feet barely touched the floor as she flung herself across the bed, praying that Lincoln wouldn't answer first.

When she snatched up the receiver, she didn't care that the bottom of the pink Princess phone cracked when it fell off the nightstand and crashed to the floor. Or that the trolls flew everywhere. All she cared about was ripping through the mass of tangled phone cord knots to get the receiver to her ear.

"Munro residence," she said as the cord finally stretched far enough. Her voice was calm but every pulse of her heart pounded against her temples. "Jessica Daniels."

"Do you have what we want?" It was the same raspy male voice from the earlier conversation.

"I don't trade unless Phil's alive."

The man didn't respond, but she could hear muffled noises as if he'd put the phone to his chest for a discussion. Then Phil was on the line, his voice a ghastly, broken, fast-forward version of the whiskey-smooth man she once knew. "Don't. Tell Iris to forget all this. Understand? I don't want Iris to remember. Let it go. Don't—"

The blow was audible.

Jessica recoiled and snapped her eyes shut. She opened them just as quickly when her mind had created a visual image to match the tortured voice. *Oh, my God, Phil.* Tears pricked her eyes for the man she'd known, for the man who cared more about his daughter than she'd realized, but Jessica couldn't be sorry for him now or cry for him. Or remember what it was like to be desperately afraid.

Her job was to pick up the pieces and ignore the emotion. That was a task for which she was imminently qualified. So she bit her lip until it bled, letting everything she felt slide away into a dark corner of her soul. Until all that existed was the job.

When the raspy voice returned, she settled the nonnegotiable details as coldly as any professional: Two men and Phil would meet her, she'd deliver a page of the book as a show of good faith before she saw Phil. When Phil had walked to or been put in her car, she'd give directions and the locker key for the rest of the book.

They agreed. Never mind that they had no intention of honoring their part of the bargain. Neither did she. In point of fact, they were the more honorable party in this transaction—they at least possessed what they intended to trade.

The phone went dead, but she didn't hang up. She stared at it, wondering how such a pretty pink phone—every little girl's dream—could be the instrument of evil. Right now she wanted to do two things with it—throw it against the wall; and call Sully just to hear his voice.

She did neither because she discovered she had an audience. Iris was back in the room. Jessica didn't have time to ask how much the girl heard because Iris went pale. Her mood ring turned black, and she clutched her stomach.

"Something's wrong. I can't find Lincoln. He didn't answer the intercom."

Fear descended on Jessica's shoulders like a vulture on a fence, hovering and waiting for her brain to accept the inevitable. Lincoln should have been back in the house by now. His routine was one last perimeter check at ten and then the inside of the house got his special attention the rest of the night. That was his routine last night. That's what they agreed upon tonight.

Jessica checked her watch. Almost eleven.

Where are you Lincoln?

She got up, tossing the phone on the bed without bothering to hang it up, and walked quietly to the door. Suddenly the eerie absence of sound spooked her. Reflex made her kill the light. She went still and listened, trying to isolate the sounds of the night from anything man-made. She couldn't—no doors slamming, no whistling, no rattling, no footsteps on hardwood.

When she was almost ready to give up, she heard the stair creak—the third one from the bottom. Iris heard it too. Her eyes lost their beautiful distinctive color in the darkness, but the fear was easy to see.

Jessica pointed to the phone and whispered, "Dial nine-one-one and tell them we've got an intruder. Then get yourself hidden beneath the mountain of clothes on that bed. Understand? You don't make a sound. You don't come out until I come get you."

Iris nodded.

Jessica waited until the girl had picked up the phone. Then pulled out the peashooter and exited the door into the hallway, hoping two hollow point peas would be enough. She didn't have time to get the .357 magnum from her purse. What a shame. Sully wouldn't turn up his nose at that one.

"Time's up." Sully slammed the phone down. "I'm out of here."

He stopped only long enough to scoop up his wallet and .45 automatic from the coffee table, and to collect his shotgun. There was a Remington 870 in the trunk of his car, standard issue for Jericho. But the Mossberg in his gun cabinet held another round in the magazine. Sully didn't believe in walking into a gunfight with less bullets than he absolutely had to.

It's overkill, bud. You don't know that you're going to need it, Sully's logical side cautioned as his fingers wrapped around the stock, pulling it out. *You don't know someone will go after her. Iris was probably gabbing on the phone with her friends. Jessie could've been calling home for messages. Lincoln might have a fondness for Dial-A-Bimbo.*

Logic didn't work. The humor fell flat. He was already out the door, in the car, and playing, "What if someone makes a move tonight. . . ."

He could get there in half an hour. She had Lincoln. She had that damn peashooter, and his intuition told him she knew how to use it. His only concern was, would she? Could she pull the trigger and put someone down if it came to it?

The woman who walked in the door that first night could. But the woman who kissed him. . . . That woman would hesitate, and the hesitation would kill her.

Maybe she wouldn't have to shoot anyone.

Maybe.

But every cop bone in his body was on alert. Never a good sign. He swore at the traffic light when it switched to red and then just ran it. His was the only car on the road.

Eleven o'clock was the dead of night on Jericho.

The hairs on the back of his neck stood up as he realized his unfortunate choice of words. He pressed the accelerator down; the car shot forward.

With every block his instincts pushed him harder. The need to get to Jessie increased. By the time he turned into the cul-de-sac, he was prepared for the worst. And that's what he saw.

The gate was open. A black-and-white blocked the entrance. Another sat halfway up the drive, and it looked like every light in the place was on. Ten or fifteen residents milled around in the end of the cove.

A sense of dread was fully formed in him by the

time he'd parked his car and flashed his badge at the crowd control officer, who tried to stop him. The young guy waved him through with an apology for not recognizing him and told him that Eason was the scene officer in charge. Sully nodded, not trusting himself to say much of anything.

He'd made upward of five hundred scenes in his career, but this one was personal. Professional distance evaporated, and he had to force himself to maintain at least a veneer of restraint. There were no ambulances, and no reason to sprint up the driveway. Whatever had happened was over. He was too late to do anything but pick up the pieces.

There was a tarp-covered body on the drive near the southeast corner of the house. Taking a breath, Sully stopped, hunkered down, and slowly lifted the edge.

Lincoln.

"I told them not to call you out, Kincaid. Hell, Turner could have handled this," Nick Eason complained loudly as he walked up. Turner was the funeral director, who doubled as Jericho's coroner. "Not much big-city detective manpower needed for this one. Throat's cut."

"I noticed." Sully let the insult slide.

Eason was a ten-year veteran, solid but not brilliant. The kind of tidy officer who closed cases as quickly as possible. He resented Jericho's bringing in an outside detective when they expanded the number of detective positions to two. From his point of view, the job should have been his instead of Sully's.

As Sully dropped the tarp, Eason told him, "We got another one inside."

Sully felt the darkness swirl inside his gut when the man gave voice and form to the possibility which had haunted him since turning into the cove. Waiting until he was standing, feet braced, he asked, "Who?"

"Male. Unidentified. Apparent burglary gone wrong."

Relief flared hot and quick through Sully. "The woman and the girl?"

Eason was clearly startled that Sully knew the exact number of other occupants of the house. "They're pretty much shot emotionally, but other than that they seem fine. I already got preliminary statements from both."

Finding out that Jessie was still alive changed everything for Sully. His professional distance began to return, but not his emotional detachment. This scene was still intensely personal. Sully had no intention of going through this again. Until this was over, Jessie and Iris weren't going to be out of his sight.

"Lay it out for me," Sully ordered as he strode toward the house.

Scrambling to catch up, Nick said, "This one's a no-brainer. We got forcible entry, a tampered security system, and a witness. The lady says the bodyguard popped one of two perps and then followed the second one outside when he ran. The second one got the bodyguard but was smart enough to get the hell out of Dodge after that. Probably because by that time the little girl had pushed the panic button. A separate set of alarms started going off like Fourth of July. She's also the one who called nine-one-one."

As Sully hit the front door, he barely glanced at the second body, also covered, lying at the foot of the stairs. His attention, his focus, every fiber of his being was concentrated not on what he saw, but on what he wanted. "Jessie."

"Here."

When he looked up, Sully knew what the cop in him had suspected from the moment he found Lincoln. Jessie's eyes were almost black now, intense. Nick Eason could write it off to shock, but Sully knew better. Lincoln hadn't killed anyone, because Lincoln never knew what hit him. They caught him outside, slit his throat from behind, and came after Jessie. After the damned book.

And she'd calmly blown the guy away without a second thought. There was no trace of remorse, no shadows, no need reflected in her eyes. No tears.

This was the woman who'd walked in the door that first night. She didn't need rescuing, not now and probably not ever. The innocence in her was the lie, the pretense. Sully was caught in a web spun by a woman he barely knew. *You know her*, he corrected as the weight of his knowledge settled into his gut. *You know her because that same darkness lives in your soul. The only difference is that you think pinning on a badge makes you one of the good guys.*

Iris must have heard his voice when he walked in. She came around the edge of the hall and lifted Jessie's arm around her shoulders. Seeing the two of them together, the last doubt slid away.

I know why you did it, Jessie. I know why. But you still killed a man. And you were calm enough to cover it up when there was no need. Self-defense would have been a piece of cake in this situation. Registered gun or not.

You killed a man, Jess. Now, what the hell am I going to do about it?

For a split second Jessica let the rough, needy way he said her name get inside her heart. She allowed herself to believe that he'd come for her because she needed him—not because this was his job. As the coldness that had allowed her to function began to fade, his expression hardened.

He knows, Jessica realized as apprehension and disappointment froze her again. She called herself a fool for wanting something that could never be hers.

Sully was a cop first, no matter what happened between them earlier. A better cop than the others, obviously. He'd caught the one tiny hole in her story. She could feel it in her soul. He knew, and it changed him. Changed how he saw her, and he didn't even know the half of it, she thought bitterly.

What are you going to do now, Sully?

The unspoken question stretched between them like an arrow of tension—impaling them. Finally he turned away without a word. Jessica held tight to Iris while Sully did his job. The girl wouldn't leave her side, and Jessica couldn't leave Sully. Not until she knew what he planned to do.

Beyond that horrible moment when their eyes had locked, there was nothing to indicate she and Sully were more than acquaintances. Not once did he publicly question her version of the events, or ask her more than a few cursory questions. It was all so simple, and yet she couldn't catch her breath.

Since Iris had been beneath that mountain of clothes the entire time, there were no other witnesses to contradict her story. No one saw her slip outside and put Lincoln's gun in his hand and fire it. No one watched as she dropped his empty shell casing by the body in the foyer, disposed of her own bullet casing by flushing it down the toilet, and reloaded the derringer. The bullet itself was not the problem because hollow points fragmented when they hit. She and Lincoln both preferred hollowpoints. The casing would match, and that placed Lincoln as the shooter.

Then she'd washed her hands and arms, and changed her clothes. By the time the police arrived, her story was solid, and Iris wasn't talking.

Neither was Sully. Everything they had to say to each other would be said in private. She knew that. Sully's eyes promised her that every time he looked in her direction.

He seemed content to let the cop named Eason direct everything, nodding when consulted, but otherwise standing back, biding his time. An unsettling combination of patience and anger lived in Sully. The patience made him more dangerous than the anger, Jessica thought.

Having patience didn't make the anger go away. All it did was create suspense, fool people into believing they were safe. Not her. She knew better.

When the bodies had been removed and police began to leave, she didn't feel a sense that the crisis had passed. She felt abandoned and like she was hurtling toward an unavoidable collision. Then Eason came up the stairs and gave her a reprieve.

"I don't think you or the girl need to stay here tonight. Why don't you pack a couple of bags? I'll take you to a hotel and have someone pick you up tomorrow morning to make your official statements."

"Thank you." Jessica forced herself not to sound too eager. "That's probably best."

"Yes, ma'am."

Both she and Iris were packed in less than ten minutes. When they returned to the landing with their bags, only Sully remained in the foyer. It was the first time she'd seen him without a tie, she realized.

"W-where's Officer Eason?" she asked uneasily.

"Off duty."

"He was . . . he was going to take us to a hotel."

"You got any objection to riding with me?" Sully was daring her to make an issue, to give him an excuse to take the gloves off. She didn't know whether to be glad the icy indifference was gone or frightened.

Iris hefted her bag and quietly started down the stairs. "I'd rather go with you. What if my dad calls while we're gone?"

"We can check the messages tomorrow," Sully told her. "Come here."

He met her at the bottom of the stairs so she didn't have to walk on the tarp that had covered the body. Jessica wondered if Sully had made them leave it on purpose to spare Iris the sight of the bloodstains. Probably.

The kid was as tough as they came, but Jessica knew how hard she was trying not to cry, not to think about Lincoln, her dad, what happened. When Sully picked her up to swing her past the tarp, Iris's arms went briefly around his neck as if he were an anchor. Jessica envied Iris the freedom to take comfort wherever she could find it. Especially when Sully returned the hug before setting her down.

"You comin'?" Sully asked Jessica, and as Iris stepped out the front door, he added sarcastically, "Or would you prefer to hang around until someone tries it again?"

Prodded into moving, she asked, "You think traipsing off somewhere is going to keep us safe?"

"I can guarantee it," he told her softly.

"It must be nice to be so sure of everything."

She'd reached the bottom stair. The extra few inches almost put her at eye level with Sully. Almost wasn't enough to erase her awareness of the kind of man who filled up a room, filled up her senses. This close she could see the shadows beneath his eyes and that he needed a shave. She noticed the faint scar above one eyebrow, and that his jaw was clenched.

Somehow she managed to get caught up in the details of the man, in the strength that he radiated. Heat rose up within her. It happened every time he stared down at her. Every time she remembered what he could do with his mouth and his hands.

"The only thing I'm sure of," he told her as he leaned forward, his gaze on her lips, "is that I'm a fool."

Jessica braced herself for a kiss that never landed. He pulled the overnight bag from her hand and walked away.

Disappointment billowed up, crowding out the expectation and heat. Alone in the foyer, she realized he wanted her to feel this way. He wanted her to know that there was more unfinished business between them than just the mess of Phil's disappearance or the break-in.

He wanted her to know that he called the shots.

Believe me, I'm in complete control. Jessica clearly remembered saying that to Iris. What a joke, and how right Iris's tarot cards had been. Sully was in control. He had the experience and the patience to make her life miserable. And she couldn't do a damn thing about it.

Slowly, Jessica followed them to the car. The routine was a familiar one by now. Iris in the middle, Jessica by the window, and silence all around. She broke it when she noticed they weren't heading downtown.

"Where are we going?"

Sully considered lying, but he didn't. There were

enough lies between them already. "My place. It's not the Ritz, but it'll do."

"Why?"

He'd expected an argument, outrage, a scene even. Not a simple question. But then Jessie never did what he expected. Without taking his eyes from the road, he said, "Because I want you there."

"Are you sure?"

There was such quiet desperation and need in that question, Sully wondered if Jessie realized how it sounded. This time he turned to answer her. "I guess that's two things I'm sure of."

I'm a fool, and I want you. Yeah, those were the two things.

The night began to spit rain at them. Sully switched on the wipers and wished whatever it was that drew him to Jessie could be wiped away as easily. But that wasn't possible. Hadn't been from the moment he'd touched her. And now he intended to make things worse by putting her in his house.

A roll of thunder punctuated his misgivings. When they reached the beach, lightning had split the sky too many times to count. It was going to be a long night.

They were wet by the time they made it from the car to the porch. He carried their things to the spare room. Jessie and Iris followed him slowly through the dark house. He set the bags inside the door and told Jessie, "I'll make coffee."

Translation: Change clothes, tuck Iris in, and then it begins.

Sully left them and fixed the coffee, but nursed a beer in the dark living room while he waited. His eyes were accustomed to the blackness. He preferred it. The only illumination came from the occasional flash of lightning. The drapes were drawn, but the wooden door stood open.

Jessie was easy to see when she finally came out of the guest room. She wore a long white T-shirt and dark leggings. As his gaze ran downward, he noticed she was barefoot again. He was too. His boots were the only thing he'd bothered to remove, preferring instead to sit and wait for Jessie.

Hesitantly she came forward, hand in front of her and taking small steps. "Could you turn on a light?"

"The couch is right beside you. Just sit down."

"I'm not very fond of the dark," she finally admitted as she sank into the couch, as far away from him as possible.

Sully flipped on the lamp beside him. She blinked and then focused on the beer in his hand. "I thought you were making coffee."

"I did. You want some?"

She shook her head and tackled the next issue. "The guest room bed is only a single."

"I know. You can take my room. I'll sleep out here."

"The couch isn't long enough."

"I know that too. But the chair'll do just fine. It knows me better than most people. Hell, it treats me better than most people."

He intended the insult to hit home. He wanted to prick that veneer of hers. She was so damned good at looking innocent and needy that he had to remind himself of the controlled woman who'd stared down at him from the railing earlier. That woman hadn't been vulnerable. Not a bit.

Setting the beer down, Sully hauled himself up and went to stare out the screen door. He needed distance. His shirt felt cool against his skin as the rain whipped the breeze around. Sea air and rain mixed into a clean scent that helped calm his mind. Until Jessie's soft voice reached him.

"Thank you."

As if that covered it.

Sully's patience snapped; the rage flared.

ELEVEN

Jessica held completely still as Sully wheeled around. For an instant lightning created a silhouette of him in the frame of the door. When the thunder followed, the power went out, leaving her alone in the dark with a man who knew too many of her secrets.

This moment was what people meant when they talked about hell breaking loose. Sully could easily play the devil's part.

"Thank you?" he echoed too softly as he walked toward her. The ice in his voice chilled her to the bone. "Thank you? Do you have any idea what it may have cost me to stand there while Eason fell all over himself in his haste to believe your lies? To shrug when he said that there was no need to bother with ballistics? You killed a man, Jessie, and no matter how strong the reason, we both know I let you get away with it. And all you can manage to tell me is, *'Thank you'*?"

He kicked the coffee table out of his way and pulled her up from the couch. "You're going to tell me more than that. You're going to tell me the truth. For once. Do you think you can manage that, Jessie?"

"No."

It was the worst possible answer. It was also the truth. His fingers tightened on her arms. She thought he might shake her, but he didn't. As her eyes grew accustomed to the dark, she saw the struggle within him reflected in his face. It was the same struggle she faced every time he touched her.

Issues disappeared. Anger melted into anticipation. Only hunger was left behind, fed by the memories of the last time Sully put his hands on her.

He had warned her in Houston what would happen when his anger dropped away. This time she didn't run. She needed him, his strength, something to hold on to in the dark.

She didn't want to be alone anymore. Just for a little while she wanted to be important to someone. Before tomorrow came. Before she walked into the trap she'd set for herself.

Deliberately she brought her hands up, flattening her palms against his chest and leaning forward. She saw the muscles work in Sully's neck and jaw as he grasped at the last trace of anger.

"This won't change anything," he told her, increasing the pressure against her arms, holding her back.

Yes, it will. It'll change everything.

But she didn't argue; she kept leaning, waiting for him to lose the battle that she'd already lost. As the seconds passed, she could tell his will was stronger than hers, and she finally had to goad him.

"Why don't you stop thinking about it and just do it, Sully?" she asked. "You'll feel better. I'll feel better. We'll both—"

Sully cut off the words with his mouth, his tongue thrusting between her parted lips. As soon as he kissed her, an eddy of desire rippled through her. This was what she wanted—his heat, his intensity inside her, making the loneliness go away, making her feel alive.

But it wasn't enough, he still controlled her, pushing her away, letting only their mouths mate. This time she wanted it all. When she tried to unbutton his shirt, he caught her hands and broke the kiss.

"I don't think so, Jessie. This is my show. You wanted me to 'just do it'? That's not how it works. Not with me. This is going to take a while." Sully dragged her hands behind her. "I'll tell you what I want when I want it. Those are the rules, Jessie. You still want to play?"

His voice was like quicksilver spilling through her. Jessica couldn't remember wanting anything more. She didn't trust herself to speak, afraid the yes would turn to maybe. This was the point of no return. Sully made that very plain. She took a deep breath and nodded.

When Sully saw Jessie's surrender, he smiled and let go of her. "Take off your shirt."

She cut her eyes toward the spare bedroom. "But Iris is—"

"She's dead asleep or the thunder would have woken her already. Take off your shirt. Don't tell me you're shy." His voice dropped. "We both know better. And I've already seen what's under there. I just want to see it again."

Folding his arms across his chest, Sully waited. When her hands strayed to the edge of her T-shirt, he felt his arousal jump, hardening. As she lifted the shirt, light from the storm flooded the room, and despite his control Sully had to let his breath out slowly between his teeth to keep from groaning.

She was damn near perfect if you liked your women with curves. And he did.

"The derringer's missing," he noted in a voice too husky, as she pulled the shirt free of her hair and tossed it on the couch.

"I don't usually wear it to bed." Her answer was a whisper.

"Lucky me." Sully traced the edge of one bra strap downward, over the curve of her breast to the center of the deep-cut bra. It was a shade darker than her skin and fastened in the front. One wrong move and she'd tumble out of the thing.

He let his fingers toy with the satin ribbon that disguised the hook, and enjoyed the way she caught her breath when his fingers slipped behind the ribbon. Dropping his hand finally, he said, "Unhook it. Nothing else. Just unhook it."

Because there was no light, he wasn't completely sure, but he thought her hands shook as she fumbled with the catch. Impatiently he pushed them away and popped the hook himself. Then, he started on the buttons of his own shirt as Jessie tried to figure out what to do with her hands and her eyes.

It had been a long time since he'd been with a woman who could still be nervous about something as simple as sex.

Her hands stopped their clenching and unclenching as he reached the waistband of his jeans. Her head angled down, gaze riveted. Sully pulled out his shirttail and kept right on unbuttoning. When he finished, he spread his shirt open and then reached for the edges of her bra. In one motion he peeled back the cups and brought her to him, using the bra to hold her against him.

The half shudder that accompanied her sigh as she melted into his chest almost undid him. When he lifted her chin, her eyes were closed, and suddenly it wasn't a wicked game of control anymore. Jessie wasn't playing a game. This wasn't just sex. This was real, and Sully felt a little piece of himself slip away, felt the solid ground beneath his feet become quicksand.

Jessica didn't know what she had expected, but it wasn't this. It wasn't that she'd lose herself in the feel of his body against hers. Her nipples tingled. Sensation hummed along her nerve endings, pooling between her legs. She had to close her eyes to anchor herself. To keep from asking Sully to touch her and to keep from rubbing herself against the thatch of hair on his chest.

Sully had rules, and she refused to break them.

When he lifted her chin, she knew she should open her eyes, should meet what would be a mocking gaze with a challenge of her own, but she couldn't. She wanted this to be real. She wanted to pretend that Sully felt something for her besides the lust. If she opened her eyes, she couldn't pretend anymore.

The first kiss was tender. No more than a brush of his lips. Jessica moaned in frustration. All she got for her trouble was a kiss on the shoulder as he stripped off the bra. Her hands found their way around him, mirroring the touch of his fingers as they explored the small of her back. With every stroke his mouth moved another inch along her shoulder toward her neck.

Then he covered her sides with his palms, moving them upward until his thumbs could stray beneath her arms, along the swell of her breasts. Jessica shifted her hands, sliding them along his biceps to his shoulders and exposing more of herself to his touch. His mouth found the pulse in the side of her neck, but he was obviously going to make her wait for anything else.

She wasn't sure she could. Her fingers tangled in his hair. "Sully, *please.*"

It was as close to begging as she'd ever come.

He cupped one breast, lifting it slightly, brushing his thumb across the tip as his mouth trailed down from her neck to capture the nipple. Jessica tried not to make a sound. But the best she could do was a close-mouthed moan at the first pull. His mouth was so hot, and wet, and merciless. She felt the pulse of each tug echo between her legs, felt herself growing damp.

When he took his mouth away and abruptly lifted her to carry her into his bedroom, it was almost a relief, a respite from the relentless sensation that threatened to swamp her. But the respite didn't last. Sully lowered her almost as quickly as he'd picked her up. He shut the door by backing her against it, taking her mouth roughly as he shed his shirt.

She took advantage to run her hands over his chest before he could pull them away, soaking up the texture of hair beneath her fingers. When his hands were free, he didn't stop her. Instead she felt him unfastening his jeans. A quiver shot through Jessica as she felt his hardness against her belly. The thin leggings weren't much more than a second skin.

Sully had to cut Jessie off when her hands dropped toward the opening of his jeans. He circled her wrists and returned her hands to his chest. She could touch him; she just couldn't hasten the inevitable. Right now, he was fighting with every breath to make this last.

She was magic in his arms, soft and giving—responding to his touch like she'd never been pushed to the edge before. Sully wanted that; he wanted her so close to oblivion that when he entered her, all she'd need was a nudge to send her over.

Smoothing a hand down over her abdomen, he felt her muscles tighten, but this time he didn't have to ask. She braced her legs apart, giving him access. Her pants were so thin, he could feel her heat and the pulse of her desire as he cupped her intimately. But it wasn't the same as silken flesh against his fingertips.

Tired of waiting, Sully curled his hands in the waist of her leggings and peeled them off her. Jessie's gasp was her only protest until he began to kiss her belly button, his mouth sinking lower as his hands rode her thighs upward. When he kissed the curls of her mound and used his thumbs to expose the sensitive nub, she froze, realizing at last what he intended.

But she didn't say no.

Sully swirled a circle with his tongue, only to stop because his own control began to slip as she trembled beneath his touch. The spike of passion rose in him so fast that he had to rest his forehead against her belly until the moment passed. As he retraced his path to her breasts, the hollow of her throat, and finally her mouth, Sully didn't remember ever having to hold himself back. Couldn't remember a woman who could destroy his control without ever having touched him.

That's why Jessie was dangerous. From the moment he'd laid eyes on her, she'd had the power to wreck his restraint. He'd fought emotion all his life, only to find a woman who could make him feel, make him want to lose himself inside her.

With every brush of his lips against hers, he pulled her toward the bed. He wanted to be inside that tight velvet glove before he came. Turning so that she reached the bed first, Sully let her sink back as he got rid of his jeans.

Her eyes were wide now, suddenly wary as he knelt between her legs. She opened for him, but her breathing was fast, her belly tight as he ran a hand over it. When the tip of his hardness rubbed against her silken folds, she arched her back and closed her eyes.

Still Sully held back, going slowly again, making sure she was ready for him. As his manhood teased her damp softness, he let his fingers stroke her thighs, down and up. With each circuit of his fingertips, he could feel her wetness coating him, allowing him to slip a tiny bit farther inside the velvet tightness that taunted him.

When her hips finally rose to meet him, Sully lost the battle and sank himself inside her. He heard her sharp gasp, felt the thin evidence of her virginity shred as he thrust, but by then it was too late. The damage was done and no way to repair it. Sully froze, afraid to move for fear he'd come. Afraid not to move for fear he was hurting her.

The storm that raged outside was nothing to the one that raged within him. All the signs he'd dismissed or ignored flooded through him. And so did the incredible knowledge that Jessie belonged to him and no one else. Another piece of his soul slipped away.

He searched her face, certain he'd see regret. Sully couldn't tell because Jessie's eyes were as tightly closed as before. But her hips were beginning to move, circling, pushing, experimenting—forcing him to hold her still before his last trace of control vanished.

"Look at me, Jessie," he ordered, the strain in his voice evident even to him.

She opened her eyes slowly, but there was no regret, no fear. Only passion and expectation. And trust. The combination was lethal. As he withdrew a fraction, she sucked in a breath of disappointment, not pain. When he drove back in, she exhaled in ragged relief.

"Again," she urged, her voice no more than a sigh.

With each stroke Sully withdrew a little more, let himself thrust a little harder until he felt her body pick up the rhythm. Release tantalized them, floating just beyond their grasp, coming closer each time he filled her. Never once did her gaze waver. Never once did he consider stopping. He couldn't.

Jessie's eyes finally closed again as her back arched. Her hands dug into the edges of the pillow, and she moaned his name so softly, he almost missed it. His name became a gasp, and even so, he wasn't prepared for the powerful shudder of satisfaction that shook Jessie.

Her orgasm rocked him, immersed him in pleasure that tore away his restraint. As her climax reached into his soul and tangled it irrevocably with hers, a groan ripped from Sully's throat. His own climax began to shudder through him, making him thrust fast and hard, all pretense of control gone. All that existed was Jessie, the way she still quivered beneath him, and the feel of her body around him as he spilled into her. As deep as he could get.

The rumble of distant thunder faded away as Sully finally surfaced. Reality called to him as it always had, and for the first time in life, he had to force himself to obey and pull away. If he didn't get some distance, he'd make love to her again and couldn't take that chance. He'd lost enough of himself in Jessie already.

By the time he'd dragged on his jeans and picked up his shirt for her, Jessie was curled up against his headboard, hugging the long pillow across her body for modesty's sake. The sight of her rocked him to the core. And he wanted to claim her, wanted to be inside her again. She was his. Something that was never supposed to happen.

If he needed a visual image of exactly what had taken place, he couldn't have picked a better one. There was no denying that Jessie had given herself up to him in a way that was completely foreign to her. Blindly trusting that he wouldn't hurt her.

Staggered, Sully realized that she couldn't trust him with the truth, so she gave him the only other thing she had to give. Herself. And he didn't deserve it. Jessie should have saved herself for a man who knew how to love someone. He didn't have a clue.

About any of this. And Jessie had let him walk right into the trap. Jessie had *baited* this trap intentionally. But the sexual chemistry had caught them both in its snare. She had no idea what he was capable of, no idea what she risked by stripping away the control that kept the darkness at bay.

Without a word he tossed the shirt toward her and walked out of the room. He couldn't bear to look at what he could never have. He dealt in the hard, dark realities of life. His soul contained a capacity for violence that he fought every day. He was bad to the bone, and she deserved better. Every woman did.

Jessica caught the shirt he flung at her and watched him go. He was full of anger again. She'd done the unforgiveable. She'd tempted Sullivan Kincaid to lose control. She had expected something real from him, and she got it. Now, all she had to do was hold on to it. At least in a little corner of her heart where no one could see.

Dragging on his shirt, Jessica closed her eyes and pulled the collar up to her nose. *Sully.* Every part of her body remembered his touch, the one brief moment of pain, the feel of him inside her, the incredible expression of awe and responsibility on his face when he made her open her eyes. He wanted the connection, to know there was no mistake, that she was his.

In that moment she'd felt important and safe for the first time in a long, long time. Sully had a gift for that, for creating a promise with a touch or a look. He'd keep her safe, but that promise also meant she couldn't fall in love with him. Not Sully. Oh no, the man was an island unto himself. He wouldn't allow someone to love him.

God help any woman who loved the man.

God help her because she was falling.

Jessica treasured the fleeting bond created when he came inside her. When he finally gave himself up completely to what was between them. When he needed her to anchor him and bring him home. She wanted it to happen out of bed. She wanted it for always.

She wanted the moon. She wanted the stars when hell was more likely her reward.

Making love had changed everything and solved nothing. There was still a child to protect, her father to rescue, and lies to be told. And then, when it was all over—if she was still alive, there was the truth to tell.

Sullivan Kincaid might forgive the lies, shooting the intruder, trying to rescue Phil, but he'd never forgive the past. To him she'd be a murderer. The government's killer, but a killer all the same.

There wasn't much forgiveness in Sully. Not for himself. Not for the people around him. Knowing that, she walked out of the bedroom to face the man she had fallen in love with. And she had to pretend she didn't care.

The screen door creaked behind him, but Sully didn't trust himself to turn around. The thunderstorm had passed, moving inland, trailing moonlight in its wake. He fixed his gaze on the beach, on the retreating waves that left rivulets of liquid silver on the sand. It reminded him of the way Jessie washed over him, leaving behind her mark, sensual memories he would never forget.

He almost hated her for that.

His first words were intentionally harsh. He didn't care. A dose of reality never hurt anyone; delusions, on the other hand, could kill you. They'd killed his mother. Jessie was better off knowing the score, even if he had to be a son of a bitch to get the point across.

"You're a fool if you think you can trust me with your heart."

"Well, at least you think I have one. So, I guess that's a better start to this conversation than your calling me a *heartless* bitch," she shot back.

Sully had to smile in spite of himself. He'd been so caught up in the detail of Jessie's virginity, he'd forgotten that she had some grit to go with that chastity. She used a bad news exterior to hide the innocent on the inside. He hid his true nature behind a badge and a white hat. They were flip sides of the same coin.

When he turned to face her, he leaned against the damp railing, curling his fingers around it near his hips. She had on his shirt, the sleeves rolled up and showing plenty of leg. The part of her hair was ragged, finger-combed. Irrationally, the fact that she *looked* exactly like what she was—a woman who'd just been tumbled—made him angry all over again. Reminded him that Jessie had manipulated him.

"You make a nice target in that shirt," he snapped.

"It doesn't matter. A cop's house is the last place anyone would look for me."

"Why's that?"

She pointed out the obvious. "People in my line of work tend to avoid the law."

"Oh, yeah. I forgot for a minute that you're a spy and not some dewy-eyed innocent," he said, his tone dripping sarcasm. "You'll have to excuse me if I'm a little distracted. I can't remember ever having been anyone's first." He nailed her as he added, "And I can't imagine a detail like that slipping anyone's mind, can you?"

"It didn't slip my mind."

"And yet you didn't say a word. Don't you think I had a right to know?"

"Would you have 'sullied' my reputation if I'd told you?"

Sully pushed away from the railing, angry as hell. Because she was right. He wouldn't have gone near her, and she knew it. "Dammit, Jessie, I didn't even use protection."

"My medical history is clear."

"Yeah, well, if your fallopian tubes are, too, we're in big trouble," Sully snapped.

Judging from the way her brow quirked, that possibility was one she hadn't considered. It was one that Sully had considered for years, carefully considered and rejected. Sullivan Kincaid didn't have what it took to be a father. It wasn't in the genes.

"I'm not asking you for anything," she told him quietly. "No commitment. We had sex."

Sully called her a liar with a look. Sex was only a part of what had happened between them.

"Why can't we let it go at that?" she asked.

Because Sully couldn't. He had to know. "Why me?"

TWELVE

Jessica caught her breath at the accusation Sully packed into two tiny words. Then, she wondered how to defend herself. She couldn't explain why Sully had been the only man to tempt her into bed. Not rationally.

Physical attraction was only part of the answer. The easy part. Blue eyes, great body, and a voice that registered halfway between whiskey and sex. Right now, she could add the way the hair on his chest narrowed to a thin line down his muscled abdomen. The way he looked in a pair of jeans that he had zipped but hadn't bothered to button.

Good-looking men were around every corner. But none of the men she'd met in her life had ever come close to unnerving her the way Sully did with a simple phrase or word. It wasn't his voice so much as *what* he said, and *when* he said it. None of those other men had pursued her relentlessly. She hadn't let them get close enough.

Sully, on the other hand, hadn't waited for an invitation. There wasn't any distance between them.

Never had been, not from the moment they'd measured each other across Munro's foyer. He didn't have to break down her walls because he had stepped right over them, refusing to believe they were meant for him. Those walls were for mere mortals, not for Sullivan Kincaid.

Sully chose her as much as she chose him. Intuition recognized a soul mate, even if the conscious part of the brain denied it. Yin and yang. Iris could probably explain it to him, but Jessica didn't think she could, not without revealing emotions she'd regret. He had too much power over her already for her to give him more.

Finally, she walked toward the porch railing to buy some time. The planks beneath her bare feet were cool and wet and warped in places. Even as she walked away from him, she was aware of the force of her attraction to the man. She felt like the ocean which couldn't escape the invisible pull of the moon. That's why it had been Sully and no one else. But he wouldn't like that answer, so she asked a question instead.

"Why not you?"

"Why not me?" His bitter laugh mocked the question. "Because no woman past the age of twelve has ever mistaken me for a knight in shining armor."

"Of course they haven't," she agreed hotly, stung by his sarcasm. "You're the Dark Knight, and you make damn sure anybody who gets close to you knows it. You wallow in it. Living by a code of your own, judging people against a standard even you can't possibly measure up to."

"Aw," Sully sighed, shaking his head. "Poor thing. Are you already disappointed in the knight you've chosen? I did warn you."

"Go to hell, Sully. I don't need knights or anyone else to rescue me. I take care of myself. I always have."

His voice was dangerously smooth as he responded, "That was made fairly clear to me when Lincoln got dead and you didn't."

Jessica stiffened. "I had no choice."

This time.

"Who was it?" he asked, abruptly changing the subject from personal to business. "CIA or someone else?"

"I don't know."

"Give it a shot," Sully ordered as he came to stand beside her. He propped his back against one of the support posts and crossed his arms over his chest. "I'm in this up to my neck now, and—considering what happened to Lincoln's neck—I expect a little cooperation. You can understand that, can't you?"

"Gosh, when you put it so sweetly, how could I not?" Jessica asked coldly. "If I had to guess. . . ."

"You do."

She gritted her teeth to keep from giving Sully the fight he wanted. Events had pulled her along so fast tonight, she hadn't stopped long enough to consider exactly who the guy had worked for. Her first concern had been protecting Iris, then protecting herself from being at the center of a police investigation, and lastly, dealing with Sully. There was a full-time job.

Clearing her mind, she let herself cast back over the seconds before she'd fired the gun. First impression, that's what she wanted. That first split second when he'd turned toward her, gun raised but late somehow. Angling her head upward, she made her guess. "I'd say he was a company man."

Surprise flooded Sully's expression—as if he'd been sure the intruder was someone other than the CIA. Leaning toward her, he cross-examined her like a cop. "Are you absolutely sure?"

"No!" Jessica shook her head in exasperation. "I'm not sure at all. I told you it's a *guess*. That's like a hunch. You remember what that is, don't you?"

"Yeah, that's when I think someone's lying to me, but I can't prove it."

Jessica closed her eyes, counted to ten. She was tired. It was three in the morning. Too late and too early to play word games with Sully, but he wouldn't leave her alone.

"What's this hunch based on, Jessie?"

Exhaling and opening her eyes, Jessica tried to put her flash of intuition into words and failed miserably. "It's just that he was too confident. Like he had a team backing him up and all the time in the world. It's different with freelance people. It's just . . . different."

"To risk coming after you like that— Don't you think they had to be pretty damn certain you had the book?"

"I don't know. Maybe."

"What made them believe you had it?" he pressed. "Why now? Why didn't they come after you last night? What's changed?"

"Because last night they still had places to look!" she snapped. "Now, they're running out. I imagine they didn't find anything in those boxes of files from Phil's office."

"The CIA shut down the Houston investigation," Sully told her, and paused—obviously expecting a reaction. She didn't give him one. "They called the dogs off and muzzled the media. Sounds like they don't want Phil or that book found any time soon."

"Standard procedure. They'll take care of it internally." Jessica pushed past Sully. She couldn't think with him so close, or catch her breath, not when he dropped bombs like this on her.

Lincoln might have cleared the house of bugs, but a parabolic microphone could have picked up her side of the conversation with Phil's kidnappers. Dear God, that was why they tried to kill her tonight. The company overheard her side of the dialogue, and they sent someone to stop her from trading that book. The book she didn't even have.

What have you done, Jessica? Silently castigating herself for stupidity, Jessica grabbed a handful of shirt over her stomach and forced herself to think. Her mind rapidly spun out the possibility that was most likely as she paced the length of the porch.

Plan A had been a disaster, so they'd have to drop back to Plan B. Jessica was grimly certain that they had a Plan B. They knew the swap location.

How many would they send? Probably only one, she decided. Someone good. Somebody better than good. He'd want them all in the open, so he'd wait until the deal was done. He'd take out the kidnappers first. They'd run for cover if they could, but she'd stay to help Phil, which made her a secondary target, a safe bet. Always get the runners first; the bleeding hearts second.

No mistakes this time. That's why the company would send the best they had. One hit man, no need for elaborate planning. Just four shots, and he could save Phil for last. Phil wouldn't be much of a challenge in his condition. Which meant that *three* fast shots at sitting ducks were all her opponent had to make.

She had to make those same shots . . . only one of her ducks wasn't in a row. No matter—it's a piece of cake, she told herself. Focus, concentrate, and squeeze off three rounds. Six seconds, maybe five. All she had to do was spot the "cleaner"—the CIA operative—first. That's all.

Jessica wanted to laugh. It was amazing how a mind could take an impossible problem and selectively re-work it so that it didn't seem so impossible. If he got off the first shot, she'd at least have sound to locate him. Her only advantage was that the cleaner had no idea Jessica Daniels was Gemini, one of Phil's "boys." Maybe he'd make a mistake and show himself too early, dismiss her as an opponent.

Yeah, and maybe they'll send two instead of one.

"Jessie?" Sully's worried question from behind her dragged her back to the present. "What is it? What's wrong?"

Tomorrow would have to take care of itself, she decided. She had no choice. She'd made Iris a promise to bring her father home. She'd die before she broke that promise. Dying was a distinct possibility.

Facing Sully, she took a deep breath and confessed, "I seem to have made a small miscalculation."

Her face was so pale, Sully thought it might be a trick of the moonlight. When she hugged herself, he knew it wasn't. He'd taken a step toward her before he stopped himself, remembering how easily she lied. Jessie had an agenda and falling into bed with her hadn't changed that. Pale or not, she still wasn't telling him the truth.

Now that he was a little closer, he could see the determined set of her mouth. She had plans within plans. With Jessie, unwrapping one layer only led to another.

"What miscalculation?" he asked.

"How tired I am. I can't do this now. Okay?"

"We're done anyway."

"No, we're not." Jessie shook her head in disgust. "We won't be 'done' until you decide what you're go-ing to do about all this . . . about me. Nothing is what it seems. The boat is rocking, and you can't stand it."

"I'm funny that way. I'm an officer of the *law*."

"You're not a cop," she told him as she stepped past him. "You're judge and jury, Sully. You like good and evil neatly labeled so you can hate the one and admire the other. Sad fact is, most people are both. You've got to take the bad with the good. Or you'll end up with nothing at all."

Sully turned on his heel to stare after her. "How many fortune cookies did you have to go through to come up with that pithy little philosophy?"

"Just a lot of bad years and one smart cookie—Madame Evangeline. The kid's spooky with a deck of tarot cards. She nailed me. She sure as hell nailed you." Jessie dragged open the screen door and got in one parting shot before she left him standing on the porch. "Of course, no one bats a thousand. Iris was a little vague about exactly what went wrong between you and your father. Night, Sully."

He blamed the cool night air for the gooseflesh and the prickling of the hairs on the back of his neck.

At the scream Jessica's eyes flew open, and she sat bolt upright in bed, trying to orient herself. For a moment she thought the nightmare had awakened her. The night was gone, but the room was still dim. It wasn't Utopia, she realized; it was Jericho. This was Sully's room.

As she sucked in air to settle her pulse, the sound came again. It was an eerie muffled half cry, half wail. Not the nightmare scream at all, but disturbing—

Iris.

Flinging the covers off, Jessica hit the door at a

run. The living room was empty. The spare room door was closed, and Jessica held her breath as she opened it. Dammit! Iris wasn't in the bed.

Surely they didn't find us already. Surely they wouldn't take a little girl just to get some leverage. Would they? Of course they would.

Heart in her throat, Jessica sprinted toward the screen door. "Iris!"

"Whoa!" Sully grabbed her as he rounded the corner of the kitchen and hauled her back by her arm. "What's the rush?"

"Sully! Something's wrong." She tried to drag her elbow away from his grasp. "I heard someone crying, and now I can't find Iris."

"Whoa, whoa, whoa. Settle down. She's on the beach." He held a mug dripping sloshed coffee away from him. "I just came back in for a refill. You probably heard the gull."

"A gull?" All the air whooshed out of Jessica, deflating her terror.

"I've got a crazy one nesting underneath the house." Sully let her arm go. "She's got a real nasty cry if you aren't used to it."

"It was a bird? My stomach is in a knot, my heart is in my throat, and it was a *bird*?"

"'Fraid so."

She took the cup of coffee out of Sully's hand and downed half of it before she'd made it out the door. The caffeine began to calm the shakes which came from trying to operate on four hours of sleep. The normal sounds of non-crazy gulls and terns blew away the last of the fear and cobwebs. Still, her heart constricted when a small figure walking in the surf turned to wave at her.

If anything had happened to Iris. . . .

Sully watched Jessie's knees give out, and she sat down abruptly on the porch steps. Last night's break-in had obviously scared her more than she let show. Layers and layers, Sully reminded himself.

Her shirt and bra had been gone last night when he went back in the house. But this morning she still had on his shirt; she hadn't changed except to add the leggings. Sully was swamped by a feeling of intimacy. Jessie had invaded his life without trying. She occupied his dreams, slept in his bed. Now, she sat on his porch, drinking *his* coffee from *his* mug and wearing *his* shirt.

Had it been any other woman, he would have been itching to pack her into a car and wave good-bye.

The part of himself he'd been trying to deny since he made love to Jessie admitted that he wanted her here. He wanted simple intimacies like the scent of Jessie on his sheets and the smile she hardly ever gave to anyone. He wanted that smile to belong to him. He wanted Jessie to belong to him.

She already does.

Only her body, Sully reminded himself, the memory still fresh and sharp in his mind. He actually had to close his eyes against the wave of desire that swept through him. Great sex wasn't enough. They both knew that. There were still secrets between them—his, hers. The longer Jessie stayed, the harder it would be to give her up.

Coming to sit beside her, Sully clasped his hands between his knees and stared out at Iris. Jessie had scooted over to give him more room, but her eyes never wavered from Iris, as if she were a nervous mother hen watching out for her baby chick.

Jessie, girl, it's all about Iris for you, isn't it? That's why you're here. Whatever you're doing is because of her.

Why can't you tell me? Why is this kid's trouble like a mission for you? You almost got killed over her.

"That's an easy kid to get attached to," he noted as Iris stopped combing the beach and tried a few back bends.

"I guess she is." Jessie looked away from the girl and studied her coffee. "If you're the type to get attached."

"You're the type all right. You killed a man for her," Sully reminded her quietly.

Her hands tightened on the mug, and she pressed her lips together. He hadn't meant to bring that subject up so bluntly, but now that he had, it was just as well. Pretending didn't make the facts go away.

"Jessie, the two of you have to go down and sign formal statements today. You think she's up to it?"

She shook her head as Iris started up the sandy slope to the house. "I think she's been through all the hell a kid can stand in the last forty-eight hours. Can we do it tomorrow?"

"Probably. But I'll still have to go in and talk to the chief. I have to tell him about Munro and the CIA taking over in Houston and hope he doesn't fire me when I ask for some time off." *And then there's the call I need to make to Utopia.* "I need to be gone a couple of hours."

Jessica turned and really looked at Sully for the first time that morning. He hadn't shaved, but he'd put on a T-shirt so wrinkled, it must have been in his dryer for days. Shadows of doubt shrouded his blue eyes, turning them gray and cloudy. Sully didn't trust her as far as he could throw her. Fair enough. She didn't deserve his trust at the moment.

Holding his gaze, she said, "And you want to know if we'll be here when you get back."

"Yeah. Make me a *promise*."

"You pay attention," Jessica whispered.

"To everything you have ever said. Or done. Make me a promise, Jessie." He lifted the coffee mug out of her hand. "You said you didn't break promises. I want you here when I get back."

"And then what happens?"

"I don't know," he answered heavily, angrily, as if unwilling to examine the future. "Deflowering virgins and bending the law are new experiences for me. So excuse me, darlin', if I don't have a copy of the playbook."

"Which of the two do you hate more?" Jessie asked before she could stop herself. She knew the answer, but something inside her wanted to hear him admit that last night shook him as much as it did her.

"I hate that you picked the wrong man." He downed the last of the coffee. "Make me a promise, Jessie, or the two of you go with me."

"We'll stay tonight, Sully, but Iris needs to check the phone messages. You and I know her dad won't have called, but I'm not telling her that. And I need to get my rental car. I don't want to leave it there," she lied to cover the fact that she had to have transportation that night. "My insurance'll go through the roof if anything happens to it."

Sully laughed in disbelief. "With everything else going on, you're worried about insurance premiums? Lord, Jessie, no wonder you have that streak of white in your hair. It's from all that constant worrying."

Iris wandered up in time to hear his comments. "Virgos are natural worriers."

"I never told you my birthday. How'd you know my sign?" Jessica asked, startled.

"Oh, I'm good at astrology. It's a gift." Iris was

smiling a little. "I can always tell someone's zodiac sign. Sully's a Leo. His roar is worse than his bite."

"The only gift you have, Goldilocks," Sully told her as he got up, "is curiosity, which leads to poking around in other people's business and reading refrigerator magnets."

The tricky part for Sully hadn't been handling the chief or getting the time off. Munro carried a big stick in Jericho. His money had paid for any number of improvement projects. So sticking close to Iris was easy to sell from a public relations standpoint. If and when Munro was found, the chief was certain he'd be grateful for all the courtesies extended his only daughter.

Calling Utopia and convincing their police chief that probable cause existed to search Jessica Daniels's residence was the tricky part. Sully mentioned Munro's disappearance, implying that Jessie was one of a number of potential suspects they were attempting to weed through. Of course he could get a warrant, Sully offered, but they weren't looking for specific physical evidence, just background information—a place to start their investigations. The lady wasn't talking. She was hiding something, and it made her look mighty guilty.

Since yesterday John Fields, the Utopia chief, had already managed to find out she'd paid cash for the land and had no visible source of income. He'd met Jessie once or twice and liked her. She was quiet. Her local bank account showed a sizable direct deposit each month from some New York bank account. He couldn't imagine her being involved in anything like this. Sure, John agreed, he'd check the residence and phone back.

So, now Sully waited. His "couple of hours" stretched to three before the call came.

"What'd you find, John?" Sully asked as he closed the door of the small office he shared with the other Jericho detective.

"Well, you were right. Ms. Daniels is hiding something all right, but I don't think it's got anything to do with the mess you got over there in Jericho. Her last name's not Daniels."

"That doesn't surprise me."

"This will. We found some old high school yearbooks, and a family scrapbook. She's Jessica Dannemora. Guess she couldn't bear to part with everything. Couldn't bear to be who she was either, so she changed her name."

Jessica Dannemora. Sully tried to make some kind of connection to the name and couldn't. "That's all? She's living under an assumed name?"

"Hell, you're probably not old enough!" John exclaimed. "Lord, I guess it's been fifteen years ago, maybe more. It was one of the biggest manhunts we ever had in Texas. Every county was beating the bushes when those little girls were kidnapped."

Sully closed his eyes as dread rumbled through his gut. He could feel the rage already coiling within him. He didn't want to hear this. But he didn't have a choice. He had opened Pandora's box.

Jessie, girl, this is what you don't want anyone to know, isn't it? Her comment about it being sixteen years too late for a guardian angel came back to him.

What happened sixteen years ago?

Puberty.

Such a snappy answer. Such a horrible reality.

"How old was she?" Sully asked.

"Just short of their thirteenth birthday if I recall."

Iris's age. No wonder Jessie came out of retirement.

"You said, 'girls.' Sisters? Friends?" Sully wondered, eyes still shut as he leaned his forehead into the palm of his hand.

"Twins. Identical twins. Jessie and Jenny. From up around Dallas-Fort Worth. Their bastard of a father wouldn't agree to negotiate the ransom. He had more money than Midas, and he wouldn't even pretend to pay so the FBI could set up a sting. Made us all sick. He insisted the bureau and local police do their jobs and find those girls. Like we weren't trying. Can you imagine?"

"No." Sully thought he might be ill.

"The kidnappers got a little pissed off." John intentionally understated the situation. "According to Jessie, there were two of them. They killed Jenny, thought it might soften Dannemora up some. Of course, Jessie didn't wait on her daddy to save her."

Go to hell, Sully. I don't need knights or anyone else to rescue me. I take care of myself. I always have.

"What happened?" Sully opened his eyes and braced himself.

"She killed one of them. Stabbed him and got away. That kid had to have some kind of courage." John exhaled a breath of admiration. "They kept the girls together for almost two weeks in a dark basement. Windows were bricked in. The place was isolated. Jessie was in there another couple of weeks after they killed her twin."

I'm not very fond of the dark.

The image of Jessie, alone and terrified, haunted him. He remembered leaving her in the driveway that night he'd wanted to turn around. Remembered leaving her after they made love. Never once did she ask him to stay. Jessie wouldn't. Jessie didn't expect anyone to come for her or to stay with her. She expected to be alone in the dark.

A tingle crawled up Sully's spine. She wouldn't want or need his help in finding Phil Munro. She expected to do everything alone. He remembered the odd phone call from Texacon. The wheels were already in motion; he could feel it. And he'd been stupid enough to let her out of his sight this morning.

That wouldn't happen again.

Sully had one more question. "What happened to the other kidnapper?"

Sully didn't take another easy breath until he saw the midnight-blue sedan parked in front of his house. The weight on his chest lifted as he realized she'd at least kept her promise. Until he noted that the car was parked on the street. Jessie was either a considerate house guest or she didn't want her car blocked in. He grimly guessed the latter.

What do you need your wheels for, Jessie? He had a guess about that too.

The moment Sully got out of the car, an unexpected shriek of laughter caught his attention. Instead of going up the wooden steps in the front of his house, he traced the sound around to the beach. Stunned, he discovered the normally quiet Iris screaming with laughter and tearing back toward the waves, pursued by three kids, who had to be siblings.

"Doesn't look much like Iris, does it?" Jessie's soft voice drifted down from the porch above.

Her vigil didn't surprise him. He assumed she'd be watching the girl like a hawk. In Jessie's mind twelve-year-old girls needed protection. They got abducted and abandoned. Who could fault her logic?

Sully loosened his tie and turned around, staggered as always by his physical reaction to her. Jessie was about as far from maternal as a woman could get. She had on a skimpy little sundress that floated around her body, barely covering the essentials. The late-afternoon sun slanted across her, revealing that she had next to nothing on beneath that dress.

Clearing his throat, he jerked a thumb over his shoulder. "That's not the somber kid I left with you this morning. What happened?"

"Kids on a beach. Doesn't take long to make friends. Especially when you're scared to death and desperately need to be normal for a while."

Yesterday he wouldn't have noticed the empathy that underlay her casual explanation, or the hint of sadness in her eyes. Yesterday he didn't know Jessie's secret. Today it made all the difference in the world. "What did you do?"

"Nothing." Jessie leaned against the post and carelessly slung her arms around it like it was an old lover. "The other kids saw her on the porch. Their mom came over. I liked her, and we agreed to take turns watching them."

"I don't mean that." Sully climbed the steps, waiting until he got to the top one before tugging the tie all the way off. Waiting until he was eye level with her before he asked, "What did you do when you needed to be normal for a while? How did you forget that you were Jessie Dannemora?"

THIRTEEN

Jessica recoiled as if he'd slapped her. The sting was hot and sharp and deeply felt. One by one Sully had managed to uncover her secrets, dragging them out like trophies. He'd had to dig deep for this one. She should have realized a thorough cop like him with connections would figure out a way to get impossible information.

Unless— Involuntarily she cut her eyes toward the beach and Iris. Sully spent time alone with her this morning.

"Iris didn't say anything," he assured her, anticipating the unspoken question. "But I take it that she knows?"

"The name. That's all, I think. It was in that damned file." Slowly recovering her composure, Jessica added, "I didn't change my name to Daniels until after I started working for Phil. Dannemora was too recognizable."

"You sure that was the only reason you changed it?" His voice was so soft, so understanding that she wanted to scream.

God, she couldn't stand the sympathy in Sully's eyes. She liked the anger better. She didn't want pity, didn't deserve pity. She was alive; Jenny was dead.

"Sully, it's the past. I'm not that little girl anymore. Let it go. It doesn't concern us."

"Oh, yeah. It's the past, all right. That's why you put your butt on a plane the minute Iris phoned you. It's so much in the past that you still can't stand the dark. You could have taken your name back when you retired, Jessie. But you didn't. What happened to you is *not* safely tucked away in the past. Not by a long shot!"

"What difference does it make? So, you know my real name? What does that change? How does that make things *different*? How?" She flung the questions at him like rapid-fire challenges, without giving him time to answer.

Part of her wanted to believe that she was more than a quarry to him, but the practical part of her believed Iris. Sully was a hunter seeking prey. Pursuing the truth was what he did; he couldn't help himself. Sully didn't care. He wouldn't *let* himself care. God forbid there should be a chink in his armor.

"Hey, Sully! Look!" Iris called, snapping the tension in the air. "I've got friends! I told them you were a cop. They didn't know that. They didn't even know you lived here. Don't you ever go out on the beach?"

They came pelting up—three redheads and Iris, all wearing the official beach uniform of an oversize T-shirt on top of a bathing suit. The new kids' eyes widened respectfully at the sight of Sully. They started at the toes of his cowboy boots and worked their way up in awe. The fact that he was standing above them only added to the impression that he was a mountain.

Iris didn't bother with the inspection. "Jessie,

please can I go next door? They have a Jaguar game system. Please. Just for an hour. I'll be back for dinner. Please."

Jessica lifted her eyes to Sully's. An hour ought to just about do it. "Sure. Have Mrs. Hammond wave at me so I know it's okay."

The kids were gone so fast, they could have been Saturday morning cartoon characters zipping off in a cloud of animated dust. Kim Hammond came to the door a second after the horde disappeared inside. She was laughing as she waved. Jessica took that as a good sign and waved back.

"Okay," she said to him as she checked her watch. "You're on the clock. What do you want to know, Sully? You want the tabloid version? The police version? My father's version? If you can tell me why any of this makes a difference, then maybe I'll know what to tell you. Because right now, I don't have a clue about why you had to poke around and bring this up."

"Maybe," he said, eyes narrowing, "I brought this up because I wanted you to know that you don't have to do this alone anymore."

Her stomach plunged as if she'd taken a nasty bounce on the highway. "Do what alone?"

"Whatever it is that you think you have to do."

Jessica walked away, hardening her heart to the sincerity in his voice. She could feel the tears stinging her eyes. This was a bad conversation going nowhere. The only one she could rely on was herself. She couldn't forget that. Sully didn't mean it. He couldn't. He didn't know everything.

"I changed my mind," she said curtly. "I don't want to talk about this."

"Why? Because you're afraid I'll figure out why you're doing all this? Why you're secretly hatching some plot to save the day and rescue Phil? Is that what you're afraid of?" Sully asked as she pulled open the screen door. "Like I don't already know!"

Jessica stopped, goaded into reply. "You don't know anything."

"I know this plan of yours has to be some misguided attempt to make up for surviving your sister. It doesn't take Freud to figure this one out, Jessie!"

"Freud's the only thing I haven't tried. You see, I didn't just survive my sister, Sully. I killed her."

Stunned, Sully backed up a step, at a loss for words, just as she intended. Then, Jessie disappeared inside the house—queen of the exit line once again. Sully dragged his hand through his hair, tugging at the back a couple of times before he went after her. He found her in the kitchen, calmly washing her hands, or so he thought. Until he saw how tightly she had them gripped as she worked the lather over and around her fingers.

"You want to try that last bit again?" Sully ordered, hanging on to his temper by the thinnest of threads.

"Get a dictionary. Look up the big words."

Sully jerked her away from the sink, not caring that her soapy hands dripped water over the counter, on the floor, on him. "Save me the trouble. You explain it."

"What part didn't you understand?"

"The part about how you could kill, not just your sister, but your *twin*. You got me for a minute, I'll admit it, but the fun's over now. I know you, Jessie; I've been inside you. I know what you did to protect Iris. You'd give your life for someone you loved."

Her odd half smile alarmed him, dredging up an emotion very close to fear. She was going to give him the explanation he demanded, and he wasn't going to like it.

"One of the men came down into the basement—" She swallowed and turned back to the sink, obviously gathering herself. After she'd rinsed her hands and dried them, she exhaled audibly and faced him again.

"He . . . uh, he said that our father wasn't respecting them. And that they were going to have to convince Daddy." She stopped for a second, rolling her lips together before beginning again. Her voice was so soft, like it came from another place inside her. "They were real sorry, he said, but our dad just wouldn't talk about paying the money. The guy apologized a couple more times. Really, really sorry, he said. Then, he called my name. *Jessica, come here.*"

Her whisper chilled him, made him want to hold her tight, keep her safe. When Sully tried to pull her into his arms, she twisted away. Like everything else in her life, she was determined to do this alone. He let her go, conscious of the darkness swirling in him, the overwhelming need to punish the men who had done this to her. It was so easy to hate, especially when there was reason to hate. Loving somebody was harder. That hurt a lot more.

Right now he hurt like hell for Jessie.

"*Jessica,*" she whispered again, and then the first tear rolled down her face. "See . . . I pretended he wasn't really calling me. I didn't want to go. I didn't want to die. And we *knew*—Jenny and me—we knew exactly what he was going to do."

She made eye contact for an instant, as if she needed to reassure herself that she was in the "now" and not the "past." Jessie calmly licked the tear off the corner of her lip as it finally trickled down far enough. "They told us every day—'If your father doesn't pay, we'll have to kill you.' So when he came downstairs and called my name, I froze.

"I couldn't make myself move. I thought maybe—just maybe—if I stood real still, he wouldn't see me. I didn't get why this could be happening. I was twelve years old, and this man was going to kill me because my father didn't love me. Helluva note, huh?"

Jessie hugged herself. Sully's hands fisted with the effort to keep them at his sides and off of her.

"Do you know what that feels like?" she asked. "To know that no one cares enough to save you? That no one will come for you? To wonder every day if this is the day you're going to die?"

Sully knew what it felt like. He knew how powerless it made him feel. How terrified. He knew how many times he'd tried to become invisible. How he made bargains with God and finally stopped because He never listened, and your father beat you anyway.

"Then that day comes," Jessie continued, nodding her head as if telling herself to just get through it. "And he calls your name. I wasn't brave. I didn't go to him. I wasn't a coward. I didn't try and run. I was nothing. I just stood there. And then the man got mad because he couldn't tell us apart."

"No." Sully wasn't certain if he thought it or felt it or said the word. All he knew was that he didn't want to hear the rest. He knew where this was going. But Jessie didn't stop. She was going to say it all. Every bit. Until she owned his heart.

"He swore at us and grabbed Jenny. And I stood there. She never said a word. She was always the good one, the strong one. And he took her away, and then she screamed. I still hear it at night." Jessie lifted her chin and met his gaze squarely. Her eyes swam with unshed tears, but not another tear dared drop. "Now, you tell me I didn't kill Jenny."

Jessica waited for revulsion to creep into Sully's eyes. Every nerve in her body felt raw and exposed. She'd finally said aloud what she'd never told another living soul. No more pretending. No more waking up and hoping it was a bad dream. The words made it finally truly irrevocably real.

I'm so sorry, Jenny. I love you forever. The tears fell, but she refused to brush them off. No ploys for sympathy. No excuses.

When Sully pulled her into his arms, the first sob escaped. Jessica caught it and sucked it back inside. It wasn't supposed to be like this. It wasn't supposed to be simple. *Don't do this to me, Sully. Don't offer me what I can't keep.*

"Shh," was all he said before he kissed her forehead, then each eyelid, and the corner of her mouth. "It's over."

Comfort became need. Need became passion.

Jessica tasted the salt of her own tears on Sully's mouth as it covered hers, and she felt the restraint in him. She didn't want restraint. Not now. Not ever again. Not when Sully kissed her. She wanted him strong and hard inside her. She wanted to be a part of him; him a part of her. For just a little while she wanted someone to love her again.

Sully gave up trying to hold back when Jessie rose to match her body to his. The flimsy sundress was as substantial as a spider web. Every inch of her curves pressed against him. Groaning at the urgency building within him, he gathered up the material of her dress until he could get his hands on her panties.

"Jessie," he whispered against her mouth, his voice

and body both tight with need. Only her panties were in the way.

"Do it." Her answer was more a sigh than real words.

One good tug was all it took, and he tossed them aside.

Her hands were already working his belt and zipper. By the time she freed him, Sully thought he might lose his mind. His hand floated over the warm skin of her rump, over the plump curves, down the backs of her legs. Then he picked her up, lifting her, spreading her thighs until she wrapped them around his hips. And then he entered her.

Sully closed his eyes against the pleasure of sinking himself into Jessie. He didn't imagine he'd ever get used to the idea that she was his. Capturing her mouth again, he let his tongue do what he feared to do with his body until he had regained some control. But soon even the wet warmth around him wasn't enough, he had to stroke. The table was closest. It'd have to do.

When Sully settled her against the cool, smooth oak, Jessica gasped, not from the cool surface but from the way he withdrew and pushed into her again hard. There was no seduction between them, just a rough need to feel and be felt. This time she didn't close her eyes. This time Sully became her anchor, someone to hold tight as each thrust took her breath away and sent her spiraling toward completion.

Sully felt her muscles tighten around him each time he drove into her, as if she was trying to hold him inside, trying to take him with her as she spun over the edge. He fought her, fought the hunger in her eyes that begged him to finish it. This was too quick, too hard, too satisfying. Sully groaned because she wrest his climax from him before he was ready. As her trembling began, he plunged into her and came.

When it was over, Sully pulled away from the intimacy, but rested his forehead against hers. Making love to Jessie was like running a marathon and then believing he could do it again. Physically he probably could, he was growing hard already, but emotionally he wasn't so sure. There had been pure need between them, like drowning victims clutching anything they could find to stay afloat.

Stepping away, Sully turned his back to give her time to pull herself together as he straightened his own clothing. When he finally faced her again, she was tossing what he assumed was the torn underwear in the trash. Sully rubbed a hand across his face as he realized how rough he'd been. Jessie was new to this, and he'd ignored that fact. No matter that her need matched his or that she had initiated it.

They were so much alike. Both with childhoods no child should suffer, much less survive. And Jessie was a survivor. No doubt about it.

"I need to change," was all she said, but her eyes were filled with doubt again. She had drawn back into that place where she stood alone and was too afraid to ask for more. Sully knew that place all too well, but he let her go without a word.

When she returned, she had on blue jeans, tennis shoes, and a black shirt. The veneer of toughness was back as if she'd made hard decisions that had to be kept.

"You've already talked to them, haven't you?" Sully asked, but it wasn't really a question. As he laid out his suspicions, he shoved away from the kitchen doorway and walked into the center of the living room. "They called the night Lincoln was murdered. Am I right?"

Jessica didn't answer. What was there to say? Only more lies. None that he would believe.

"*Am I right?*" He didn't raise his voice, but the words were deafening, compelling.

"They called. Phil for the book."

"*Jesus, Jessie!*" Sully paced a circle, coming back to stand in front of her again. "Why didn't you tell me before now?"

"Men ask such stupid questions." She shook her head at the masculine peculiarity. "Because you'd try and stop me. Or go with me."

"You're damned right," he exploded. "You got no business doing this. Spying on people and picking locks for the government is one thing, but you can't do this. You aren't trained for this."

She let that pass without correcting him. "If I don't go, they're going to kill him."

"*If you do go, they're going to kill you!*" When she didn't dispute him, he sighed, visibly making an effort to control himself. "Do you even have the book?"

"No."

He grabbed her shoulders. "Listen to me, Jessie. Killing an intruder who is threatening you isn't the same as cold-bloodedly killing someone."

"Really?" she said sarcastically, as his deadly earnest gaze bored into her. "I'll try and remember that."

"Remember this—you don't have the book. You'll have to take them out before they realize that fact. You'll have to stand there, look them in the eye, and kill them."

"Seems reasonable."

His grip tightened painfully. "All you have are two shots in that derringer. Do you understand what I'm saying? Is any of this getting through to you? They have to be dead before they hit the ground."

"If I don't go, they'll kill Phil," she repeated softly. "I can't walk away from this. And you know why."

"I don't give a damn about Phil! He's not the one I care about. They're going to kill him anyway. They're going to kill *you* anyway!"

He's not the one I care about.

Jessica felt that admission slide into her, warming her. Sully didn't even comprehend what he said. But it was enough, more than she thought she'd ever get from him. It was something real to keep until she destroyed it. She couldn't let herself forget what she was, and that she'd have to tell him.

"You don't have the book," Sully pointed out again, enunciating each word as though he wasn't certain of her understanding. "They aren't going to be fooled by something you've jury-rigged. Phil is going to have to confirm what's in it, what's on each page, how it's set up. It's not going to match what he says. Jessie, listen to me."

Each word got progressively louder. "Neither you nor Phil will last ten seconds if you can't produce the real book!"

In the silence that followed, Iris's hushed voice reached them. "I can give you the book. I didn't know you wanted it. You never told me."

In unison, Sully and Jessie turned to the screen door, gaping at her. Iris felt only the briefest sliver of guilt for eavesdropping on their fight. It wasn't her fault. She would have walked away; she was going to, but then Jessie said that part about her dad being killed. That froze her in place, her hands perched on the crosspiece at the middle of the screen as she prayed she had misunderstood somehow.

But she hadn't, and then she realized all they needed was the information. Relief flooded her. That was all? she thought. That was so easy. Her dad would be safe. Everything would be okay again.

When she spoke up, they turned, waves of disbelief rolling toward her. Then anger.

"I thought—I thought you'd be happy. Doesn't this fix everything?"

Jessie pushed past Sully and came to the door, opening it and drawing her inside without a word. As soon as Iris felt her touch, she could tell the anger wasn't for her. Jessie shut the wooden door behind them and asked, "You said all you ever saw were the files. You said that on the phone. I asked you if you'd seen a book like that, and you said no. I asked you."

"There aren't any files." Guilt pinched again. "I didn't tell you that I knew about the book because I thought you wanted to use those other people, and I didn't want to. They didn't feel right. Except maybe one, but he's new and kind of young, and—" Iris rushed to explain because the expression on Jessie's face just kept getting worse with every word. "—Daddy always said that it took a while before he knew if he could trust someone to get the job done. And, anyway, he always said that you were the best of the bunch."

"Oh, my God."

"It's okay, Jessie. I'm sorry I didn't tell you. I didn't know we needed it to get Daddy back. Really, I didn't. Daddy told me never to tell anyone. All the time he tells me that. It's our secret. No one can know. Not even Rosa."

"How long have you known about it?"

"Since I was eight. I help him keep it all straight. It's how I know I'm important to him."

In that moment Sully decided that if Phil lived through this, life was going to change in the Munro household. Jessie turned away from the girl and looked at him in dumb horror. He knew what she was thinking. The same thing that he was thinking. What kind of monster puts his own child in danger and calls it love?

Unfortunately they could both answer that question from personal experience.

"Iris," he said, "can you get to the book tonight?"

"I don't have to go get it."

"You carry it with you?" Sully asked in surprise.

She nodded her head and then pointed at her temple. "It's not really a book. It used to be, but I've got a good memory, so it's up here. All of it."

Neither Sully or Jessica wanted to believe what Iris said so confidently. The concept was appallingly obvious and absolutely hideous to contemplate. Hesitantly Jessica asked, "A photographic memory?"

"Yeah, I told you I had a good memory the night I did the tarot reading. Remember? You wanted to know how I knew all those cards."

A memory flooded Jessica, but it wasn't of that first night in Jericho. Phil's voice and last words on the phone drifted through her mind and took on new meaning. Horrified at the choice they faced, Jessica turned to Sully. Her hands were shaking and cold. The words came out before she could censor them.

"Phil doesn't want her involved, Sully. I made them let me talk to him. He told me to let it go. He doesn't want her to remember. He doesn't want us to save him. That's what he meant."

"No!" Iris backed away from her like a scalded dog, betrayal in her eyes. "We have to go. You said they'd kill him if you didn't. I heard you. You said it."

"Your dad—"

"Needs me. You promised to help me. You said we'd give them anything they wanted. Anything. If I don't go, they'll kill him." Panic fueled Iris's anger at Jessica's silence. The sunburn on her cheeks disappeared as emotion reddened her entire face. "You aren't going to let me help, are you? *Are you?*"

There was no need to look at Sully again, to ask for support. This decision was hers alone. And the answer was no. How could she give them the child to save the father?

"No, we'll do it my way."

"Sully said we can't fool them. It has to be real." Iris went to him and begged, "Tell her again. Please. You can make her understand."

Jessica cut him off. "It won't make any difference."

The finality of her tone got through to Iris. She whipped around. In a voice as cruel as anything Jessica had ever used on her own father, Iris said, "If Daddy gets killed, it's your fault, and I'll hate you forever."

"Fair enough." Jessica refused to crumble. She couldn't. In forty-five minutes emotions would get her killed. Right now her focus had to be on making those three shots.

"I hate you now." Iris ran to the spare bedroom and slammed the door so hard that even Jessica's teeth shook. When the vibration subsided, she let out the breath that she'd been holding.

Jessica wasn't certain how long she stood there, recovering, before Sully came to her. As he tilted up her chin, she could hear the normal world outside—a car honking in the distance, the Hammonds' ATV humming, the dog barking as he chased the kids who cut donuts in the sand. All of her life she'd wanted that normalcy. Just a little piece of land somewhere, neighbors.

"You can't do this either," he said. "It's time to call in the professionals. Let them handle it."

"They are. Don't you get it yet, Sully? That's what I am. A professional killer."

"Stop it, Jessie. You had to kill the man who abducted you, and you had to kill to save Iris. That doesn't make you a professional."

"No. What makes me a professional is that I kill for the government. You see, Sully, that's what I do. That's what I am. The fairy tale you've been spinning about how I sneak into buildings and break codes is a fantasy. The reality is that I kill people. Everyone in Phil's book kills for the government. I just happen to be the best of the bunch."

FOURTEEN

Her blunt confession conquered Sully's denial before he could even voice it. By the end there was no need. Certainty had settled around him like a shroud, swallowing all emotion save the anger. Anger was safe, familiar. Instead of the heat he expected, this anger was cold and bitter in his gut. In his heart.

All the inconsistencies suddenly wove themselves into a pattern. Layers and layers—tough, soft, innocent, deadly. Jessie had played him for a fool from moment one. Always offering just enough to keep him interested, just enough to lead him down the garden path. Finally offering even her virginity. And the hell of it was that she'd never pretended to be innocent. He made that judgment call all by himself.

"Why?" That covered just about everything he wanted to know. He didn't care where she started.

"Because Phil Munro made me an offer I couldn't refuse."

The last piece of the puzzle slipped into place for Sully. "He found the other kidnapper when the police couldn't."

"Bingo. Phil Munro recruited me when I was only twenty years old. He showed me a picture of the second kidnapper. I'll never forget that face. Then Phil asked me if I wanted to *finish* it. Such clever wording, don't you think?"

Sully hated that he understood too clearly how much that could tempt her. Half an hour ago, he'd wanted to get his hands on that man, too, so that it would be over for her. That was before he knew Jessie could damn well take care of herself.

"He may have dangled the carrot," Sully told her, "but you're the one who said, 'Yes.' "

"What would you have said, Sully?" Jessica had finally lost some of the tough edge. "Would you have turned the other cheek? I couldn't. An eye for an eye. A life for a life. Phil sold me a bill of goods about justice, and I bought it. All he wanted was my soul."

"Every bit of it."

"No, I kept a piece. At least that's the lie I told myself. I turned down more jobs than I took. No women. No children. I took out the trash. Drug lords who peddled crack to kids younger than Iris. International terrorists who blew up whatever they felt like, no matter how many innocent people were killed. Cartel enforcers. Trash. The real bad guys the world could live just fine without."

"What happened? Run out of bullets?"

"Go to hell."

"You first." He regretted the words as soon as he said them. By walking into the trap set by Phil's kidnappers, that's exactly what she intended to do. "I didn't mean that."

"Yes, you did. You hate me for holding up a mirror. We're not so different, Sully. You hunt the bad guys the same way I did, for the same reasons I did. Except you pin on a badge and let them draw first. I'm not asking you to forgive me. To do that, you'd have to forgive yourself and get rid of all that hate you carry around."

Jessica crossed her arms and said, "So I'll give you a simpler choice than forgiving me. Arrest me or get out of my way. I've got a job to do, and my lucky gun's in the other room."

"You're not going anywhere."

"Hide and watch. I know you, too, Sully. I've seen you pull back your anger when I've given you every reason to shake me. There is a line that you won't cross. To stop me, Sully, you're going to have to cross that line. You're going to have to hurt me, and you can't do it. You can hurt the bad guys, but you won't lay a finger on a woman or a child."

"Don't count on it." When she unfolded her arms and took a step, Sully realized that Jessie still didn't have a clue about him. So he gave her one; one that would stop her cold. "I killed my own father. I think I can handle you."

Jessica froze, refusing to believe that Sully could be capable of patricide. But everything she knew about him pointed toward that harsh reality—the anger, why his eyes were sometimes cold and unforgiving, why he'd said he had "more to hide than most." Iris had called him a hunter seeking prey to escape his own darkness. In her heart she knew it was true.

He had killed his father. He offered no explanation, no defense, no emotion. No plea for understanding. Sully hadn't forgiven himself. He certainly wouldn't ask it of anyone else.

"I warned you about me, Jessie."

"Maybe you should have warned your father." The taunt was out of her mouth before she could censor it

—fueled by anger and a betrayal she didn't even understand.

"I did." Only the tic in his jaw was at odds with his casual tone. "Right before I shot him, I told him to take his hands off my mother's neck. He didn't listen either. Now they're both dead."

Jessica closed her eyes against the image of his mother being choked to death in front of him. She knew all about feeling powerless and standing by while someone you loved was killed. As he finished speaking there was no regret, no sadness in his voice. Just the blackness she felt inside him. The same darkness that haunted her in the night. Opening her eyes, she wondered which was worse, which act cost a human being more of their soul—killing with passion and then feeling nothing, or killing without emotion and feeling remorse?

For a second, Jessica's anger softened, and then she remembered she couldn't afford weakness. She couldn't afford to understand. Or care. She didn't have time to absolve him. She had a job to do. Phil needed her. She couldn't let Sully tangle her up in feelings, or she'd make a mistake. Jessica took another step toward the bedroom and her weapon.

"You're not going anywhere," he promised softly as she advanced, the edge in his voice as dangerous as anything she'd ever heard. "I won't let you."

"You don't get a vote. Either hurt me or get out of the way."

"You're so sure I won't?"

"Are you kidding? I know you, Sully. It's the one thing I am sure of."

Sully wheeled with her as she brushed past, firing a question. "Is Phil Munro worth dying for?"

She halted with her hand on the doorknob. "Phil

gave me back my life when I couldn't face myself anymore. You don't just retire from this job, Sully. Your
employment is terminated with extreme prejudice.
Loose cannons make the agency very unhappy. Phil
protected me. He's the only one who ever has."

Silently Jessica added, *Except you. Even when you
didn't want to protect me, you did. You're still trying—
because you protect people. It's why you shot your father.*

"I won't leave Phil there to die," she told him. "I
can't."

Steeling herself for another confrontation with Iris,
Jessica opened the door, expecting Iris to be curled up
on the bed and crying into the pillow. Or even to catch
her eavesdropping. When she wasn't there at all, Jessica's heart leapt into her throat. She walked into the
room only far enough to see the window. It was open.

"Oh, my God. *Sully!*"

He was at the door before she could grab her purse
and check for the gun. It was still there. Relief pumped
through her for a tiny second. If Iris didn't have a gun
in her hand, maybe they wouldn't shoot first and ask
questions later.

"What?" Sully focused on her, on the gun in her
hand, and not the room.

The Colt Python had a skeleton grip—the handles
removed to reduce the weight and bulge. The snub
barrel .357 magnum wasn't a toy like the derringer. It
was lethal. She realized that seeing the gun in her hand
threw Sully. Knowing something intellectually didn't
have the impact of seeing it in living color. A picture
was worth a thousand words.

"Iris. She's gone." Jessica had to struggle to keep
the emotions from welling up and clouding her judgment. "She thinks she can save him."

"That's ridiculous." He scanned the room, finding

the window. His face was stony. "Okay, she's just run away. Probably run home. Even if she overheard us, she doesn't know where. You haven't told me."

Afraid time was rapidly running out Jessica checked her watch, trying to figure how much of a head start Iris had. Then she lifted her eyes to Sully. She needed an anchor right now; she couldn't lose Iris too.

"I didn't need to say it today. She overheard me on the phone the night Lincoln died. Even if she didn't know what it meant then—"

"She sure as hell does now. Where is she going?"

"Landreth's Marina."

"Good God, that place is practically rotting into the sea."

"Can she get there?"

"With her memory, if she's ever seen a map of the island, she'll know how to get there. It's on this side, but we can catch—Damn it all to hell!" Sully spun and headed for the door. An old red four-wheeler was always parked near the side of the Hammond house, half-covered with a tarp. The tarp was still there. A little magnetic key case had been carelessly tossed on top of it. "The ATV we heard earlier."

The beginnings of panic blossomed in Jessica, but she stated the obvious, hoping it was true. "She can't outrun us on that. Even spotting her a head start, we can catch her."

Sully turned toward her and urged her backward, down the steps and toward the cars. "We can't catch her. She can get there by following the beach line. We have to take the long way. Let's go."

She couldn't think of anyone she'd rather have backing her up, and that scared her almost as much as Iris in the middle of a war zone. "This isn't going to be clean, Sully."

His hesitation only lasted a second. "What in life is? How much time do we have before the swap?"

"Maybe twenty-five minutes. How long will it take her?"

"Even if we run every red light, she'll be there before us. Let's hope your guys are late."

"They're expecting my car," Jessica said as he veered toward his. Then she slid behind the wheel of the rental sedan, shoving aside her cell phone and turning the key. She had already tucked the gun in the back of her jeans. "These guys are never late. They're early. I figure one of Phil's team decided to give himself a promotion by snatching Phil and taking the book."

"But the suit was tougher than he looked. He wouldn't give it up."

"The *suit* was protecting his child." She braked at the corner. "Which way is the fastest?"

"Left. Then about six miles to Walker. Go right. What's the plan?"

"I think there'll be two at the swap. One in the car with Phil, and one meeting me. We draw first."

"I'll take the car. You take the guy in the open."

"No." Jessica's hands tightened on the wheel. "I need you to stay back and take the one I won't be able to see."

"A third one?"

"Yeah, we'll have company. He'll go for the kidnappers first. Then, he'll go for me, figuring he has plenty of time. He'll assume I'm a bleeding heart who'll stay in the line of fire to help Phil. So you have to get him before he gets me."

"Company? As in CIA? As in someone better than the fellow they sent after you last night?" Sully asked, and swore when she didn't answer. "Can this possibly get any worse?"

"Yeah." Jessica didn't want to think about it, but it was possible. "They could kill Iris for fun before we get there."

Iris looked over her shoulder one last time and sighed in relief. If they were coming after her, they would have already caught her. She was safe. They couldn't stop her from saving her dad.

Sand stung her bare legs and feet occasionally, but she didn't care. If she got there first, everything would be okay. Jessie didn't understand. What could happen? It was still daylight. If the kidnappers were going to kill everybody, wouldn't they have set it up for late at night? When they could get away? Wouldn't they have picked something besides a boat marina with lots of people?

At the thought of the marina, one of those bad feelings settled in her chest. Even the harmony ball couldn't dispel the anxiety that became a gnawing force inside her. She couldn't hear the chime over the rumble of the ATV. Afraid that she was going to be too late, Iris pushed the four-wheeler to go faster.

Jessie made the last turn as Sully pointed. The marina was a straight shot from here. Five more minutes. When he couldn't stand the silence any longer, Sully asked the question that loomed so large in his mind, "Why did you walk away from it?"

"Because I ran out of bullets," she echoed cuttingly, but she added, "And hate. I ran out of hate. Except for the little dab I kept for myself for what I had become. I imagine Jenny is so proud of her big sister that she could cry."

I imagine she is, Sully thought. *I always thought your angel was weeping too.* How could he walk away from the woman if every time she opened her mouth he bled for her?

"Where is everybody?" Iris whispered as she slowed the four-wheeler to a stop.

She'd never been to this marina, but she'd assumed it would be like the ones on the other end of the island. There should have been a restaurant and a fishing pier and a bait shop. There should have been a big boat supply store and a repair place. People should be coming and going.

Instead there was silence and a sign that tilted at a crazy angle. She rubbed her nose at the smell of dead fish and unkempt beach. Landreth Marina's floating boat docks jutted out into the small cove like some great sea-creature spine. The dock bays were all but empty, making the long intersecting rectangles look more like a convention of flat river barges gone aground. A graduated boardwalk led up the slope of the beach from the docks to the parking lot and a cyclone-fenced business. A faded sign on the shack advertised "Charters—whole day and half" but one of the windows was broken. She didn't guess they had many customers.

Suddenly she wished she'd taken the time to grab shoes and shorts. Wearing a bathing suit and a T-shirt seemed a stupid choice for rescuing her father. For the first time Iris began to get scared for herself as well as her dad.

Above her she heard the sound of a car, and then

she saw the bumper and trunk as it backed into one of the spaces facing the beach. The car wasn't Sully's or Jessica's. It had to be the men who had her father.

"Daddy," she whispered, her courage returning. Racing up the boardwalk, she thrust the fear away. All she had to do was tell them who she was, and everything was going to be just fine.

When she got to the top of the steps, she realized her mistake.

"Slide down." Jessica told him. "In case they put a scope on me."

Sully unholstered his gun and slid down. "I thought *your* weapon would be a sniper rifle."

"It's in the case in the backseat," she told him, "but it tends to make a kidnapper nervous when you bring a rifle to the party."

"How about our party crasher? He got one?"

"I doubt it. He's got multiple moving targets. He'll want to be close in. He'll want to hear it go down. Be able to give chase if he misses one. This is a cleanup operation. He can't afford any missed shots because the angle is wrong."

"What do you see out there?"

"Not much from this distance. Looks like some kind of boat repair place on the left. No—The sign says something about charters. Couple of cars in the lot. One of them looks like a junker. The other's a possible. Two men."

"Iris?"

"*No.*" Jessica bit her lip until the tears were from pain and not from the hollow fear that ate away her confidence. And then she blinked them away. She couldn't have them hindering her shot. "But I can't see the beach. Just the boat docks out in the bay."

"Best guess on our party guest?"

"Not the shack on the left." She moved her lips as little as possible while she talked. "Too obvious. Maybe in one of the barrels at the edge of the fence or under one of the boat tarps. Our fellow probably lost ten pounds in the heat. It's show time."

Sully felt the dip and rise of the parking lot entrance. "Angle the car and give me a three count so I can open my door latch with yours."

She didn't answer, but he knew she heard. As soon as the car stopped, she peeled three fingers, one after the other off the steering wheel. *Click thunk*. The door latches released at the same time, one noise. Hers was the only one that swung open.

"Don't you get dead on me, Jessie," Sully whispered, just loud enough for her ears. "I'm not through with you."

Jessica almost wished she hadn't heard him. This time, beneath the anger, was a promise she'd never heard from anyone before. A promise that presumed something real existed, something worth saving. That either one of them might actually have a future. *Don't make me want what I can't have, Sully. Just let me do my job and get Iris back in one piece.*

She made herself get out of the car, refusing to think about Sully or the future. Her whole world had narrowed to one objective. She couldn't hope, not and keep her mind on getting through what lay ahead. Her only focus had to be on the two men whose car doors winged open.

As the driver unfolded himself from behind the wheel, he just kept coming—like an evil clown getting out of one of those little circus jalopies. He was six six, maybe six seven, and he didn't look happy to be here. "You the lady?"

Jessica nodded, surreptitiously scanning the area for Iris. *Where are you?* For a second she let hope flare. Maybe Iris had run out of gas or gotten stuck. Then as she walked almost to the car, she saw the red ATV down on the beach. Keeping the crushing disappointment off her face, she said, "I'm the lady."

The second man got out, dressed all in black, his weapon in his hand. "We need that token of good faith."

"You'll have to write it down to show it to Phil. I memorized it because I didn't want to tear a page out of the book."

"That's not what we agreed to."

"Plans change."

"You got that right." He jerked his head at the tall man, who casually opened the back door of the car and dragged Iris out of the floorboard. "We took some life insurance. If you don't give us what we want right now, then Phil will. Just as soon as he's conscious again."

Iris was bound and gagged. One knee was bloody like she had skinned it in a fall, but she stood unassisted. The fools had no idea what they had. Not even a flicker of Jessica's concern showed in her eyes. Nor did the relief.

"Boys, boys, boys." Pretending annoyance, Jessica put her hands on her hips, letting her thumb slip into the skeletal frame of the gun and pulled it closer to her palm. As she talked, her hands circled into fists—one of them around the grip, but still on her hip. "How can Phil give you what you want? Phil no longer knows where the book is. Your insurance has expired."

Jessica prayed that Sully was watching her back because someone had a gun aimed right at her. She could feel it. All hell was about to break loose, and Iris was right in the middle of it.

Good girl, Sully thought as she left the door ajar, giving him a view of the charter business. He gave her time to draw the attention of the two men, before he moved. When he heard voices carrying toward him, he changed his position in the car.

Carefully stretching out on the front seat, he reached far enough to slowly inch open the driver's door a little farther so he could see the entire building. The fence was about twenty-five feet away. A couple of small boats were a few feet beyond that. If Jessie was right, he'd hear the shot before he saw the man.

Time seemed to crawl as he lay tensed on the seat. Waiting distorted every sound, and with every pulse of his heart he knew the first shot could be aimed at Jessie. No matter what she said about the logic of the kill that didn't mean the man would follow it. Sully arrested criminals every day who forgot logic, criminals who got their kicks from pushing their limits.

When the first shot came, instinct kicked in. Sully zeroed on the motion and sound in the blink of an eye. His target rose up out of a boat, tarp split on either side of him, attention focused on the kidnappers. The next two shots were simultaneous and belonged to Sully and the agent. A third shot was so close on the heels of the first two that it was practically indistinguishable.

Jessie, please let that be your shot. Don't get dead on me. Not now.

Sully saw his man drop and kicked the passenger door open. His next concern was for Jessie and Iris. He wasn't even out of the car before he was bringing his weapon to bear. A second later, he lowered it. Both men were down. Jessie and Iris were standing. The exhale of relief didn't make it past his mouth. The breath turned into a shout of warning as he raised his gun.

"*Jessie!*"

Jessica was pulling the gag out of Iris's mouth when she heard Sully's shout of warning.

"*Jessie!*"

Her head came up a fraction. Looking behind Iris, she saw the muzzle. The man in black still had the strength to lift his gun.

The decision was really no decision. Her life or Iris's. No contest. One was good, and one was bad. This time the bad twin would die.

Sully watched as Jessica twisted, throwing Iris out of the way. He died as the bullet slammed into her, knocking her backward. In less time than it takes to breathe, Sully knew he loved Jessie. Absolute terror ripped the secret from his soul, and it was too late.

Too late.

He fired and ran. The man on the ground didn't move again.

The words pounded through him breaking down everything he was, rebuilding what he was into something new. There wasn't any room for the past. There wasn't any room for hate. All that was left was Jessie.

When he reached her, he tried to tell himself that it wasn't a lot of blood. "You're going to be okay, Jessie. I promise."

"Sully!" Iris was crying and yelling for him. "Daddy's in the car. In the back."

Forcing himself to leave Jessie for a second, he grabbed Iris and untied her hands. "Darlin', I need your help. There's a cell phone in the car. Call nine-one-one. Can you do it? Please. Jessie needs you. Call nine-one-one, don't hang up until they tell you, bring the phone here, and then help your dad. Can you do that, sweetie? Everything's okay. But we have to call."

She nodded and ran toward the car at speed only scared children can attain. Sully peeled off his shirt and hit his knees beside Jessie. He lifted her only long enough to find the wound and use the shirt as a pressure bandage. He hadn't cried or talked to God since he was eight years old. Pride didn't matter anymore, he realized as he watched color drain from her face.

"Okay, God, You got me where You wanted me, I'm on my knees. You wanted me to forgive the past. Let the anger go. Well, I did it. Don't take her too. Don't You make me do this alone. Don't take away my anger, if You aren't going to replace it."

Sully swiped the back of his hand across his wet cheek. "Don't leave me alone. Not when I just figured out how to be a part of something. Just when I figured out what love is."

Iris came racing back, laying the phone beside him. "They're coming, Sully. They told me five min—" Iris broke off as she looked at Jessie, realizing for the first time that this wasn't a flesh wound like in the movies. Huge tears without sobs rolled down her face. "Jessie?"

"Check your dad," Sully ordered, rubbing his eyes. "Stay with him. Let me take care of Jessie."

Iris was on her knees, reaching for Jessie's hand. "It was for me, Sully. It was for me."

"I know. Believe me, honey, I know exactly why she did it. Now, go to your dad."

When she left, Sully tried one more prayer. One for Jessie, because she couldn't do it herself. He smoothed back the white streak and said, "There's a lot of good in this woman. More than in me. She hates the dark, God. At least don't leave her in the dark. She hates the dark."

Time stretched and yawned before him like an enemy. But he wouldn't give up. Not on Jessie. She was his. The only one who ever had been. She was his.

When the sound of sirens reached him, he kept trying. "Jessie, you hear that. Don't you leave me. Stay with me. I love you. You can't go."

Jessica didn't like where she was, but she didn't like the pain either. Little by little the pain was going and the place around her got lighter. But something kept dragging her back to the pain.

It was Sully, she realized.

His voice was so strong, and she grabbed hold of it, anchoring herself with it. *Stay with me.* She wasn't alone. For the first time in sixteen years she had someone to trust, someone to love.

I love you. You can't go.

Someone who loved her.

When her eyes finally opened, she wasn't at the marina. It was a hospital. And Sully sat vigil in a chair, chin on his chest. The man needed a shave, a haircut, and love. That last one she could give him. If he'd let her.

He opened his eyes, and she found herself staring into the most unforgiving blue eyes she'd ever seen. For a heartbreaking moment, she thought it had all been a cruel dream. And then his gaze softened, and he said the words as if he'd been waiting to say them all his life. He didn't even move. He just said them.

"I love you."

Something broken inside her heart was suddenly whole. She didn't mean to cry, but the tear just kind of slipped away from her as she said, "You came for me."

"And I always will, Jessie. The past doesn't matter. Not mine. Not yours. All that matters is right now, and tomorrow, and forever." He hauled himself out of the chair. "I love you forever."

"W-what?"

"I love you forever. It's what you've been mumbling for a couple of days." He kissed her finally, so careful not to jostle her, but there was still something untamed about the touch of his lips to hers. Something that would always be there between them. "Now, you try it. It doesn't hurt. Not much. I promise."

"I love you forever." So few words to say everything that was inside her heart, and yet they were all she needed.

"Forever," he echoed as he kissed her again and twined his fingers with hers. "But now that you're awake I need to take care of unfinished business."

Some of Jessica's happiness evaporated at his hard tone. "You mean explanations for the police."

He shook his head. "I took care of that while you were in surgery. They took a nasty bullet out of your shoulder. It was bad, Jessie. You lost a lot of blood. You came closer to dying than I ever want to see again." His fingers cupped the side of her neck, and his thumb brushed against her bottom lip. Sully thought he could spend the rest of his life touching Jessie. And he would. "You're a brave woman. A hero. The department is all set to give you a medal."

"For what?"

"For saving a little girl. For saving Phil. He's lucky to have an old family friend like you, you know. We would, however, prefer that you notify the police in case of any future kidnappings, but they're satisfied with mine and Iris's version of the events. Children react so unpredictably when they get ransom calls. She really should have told us sooner."

"You didn't."

"Oh, but we did. The child is an accomplished liar. I understand Phil is so grateful that he's offered to pay all your medical bills."

"Nice of him." Jessica tried to sit up but the first nasty eddy of pain convinced her that was a bad idea.

"It's the very least he could do."

"How is Iris? Really?"

"Worried about you. But fine. And she's going to stay that way." His gaze hardened. "I'm going to see to it personally. I'm going to explain the proper care and feeding of children to Phil Munro."

"That's your unfinished business?"

"Not for long. By the time I'm through with Phil, Killers "R" Us will be nothing more than a bad memory."

"Yeah, one of Iris's memories," she added softly.

"I know."

As he eased away from her, Jessica whispered, "What if he doesn't listen? What if he puts her in danger again?"

"There'll be hell to pay."

Jessica smiled and closed her eyes as Sully walked out the door. He'd be back. He loved her forever.

EPILOGUE

Protect and Serve
Jericho Island

Jack Benjamin
Chief of Police

Valerie Carson
Mayor

Jericho Island - Law Enforcement Division
2984 Front Street
Jericho Island, TX 77201

MEMO

Date: December 8, 1997

To: Jack Benjamin

From: Sullivan Kincaid

Re: Family medical leave

You told me to give you plenty of notice. Here it is.

The obstetrician just put my wife to bed for the duration of the pregnancy. She's not due for another month, but the doc says she probably won't make it that long—not with twins. He'd like to see her carry another couple of weeks if she can, so the babies would be almost full term, but Jessie could deliver anytime. I suspect she'll hang on for those two weeks. You know how stubborn she is.

When the twins arrive, I'm going to need parental leave, my accumulated personal days, and my sick days. So you'd better plan on <u>at least</u> nine weeks of downtime for me. Maybe more. I know this will be hard on the department, Jack, and I know my request is beyond the city's guideline for parental leave. But I waited a long time to start a family, and I intend to do this right.

While we're on the subject of time off, this spring I'm going to need some afternoons. I'm coaching Iris Munro's softball team.

Sully Kincaid

THE

Loveswept

EDITORS
ARE HAPPY TO ANNOUNCE
THE THREE WINNERS OF
LOVESWEPT'S TREASURED
TALES III CONTEST!

**THERESA BURCHETT
CHRISTY M. ANDERSON
LESLIE-ANN JONES**

OUR CONGRATULATIONS TO
EACH OF THESE TERRIFIC AND
LOYAL LOVESWEPT FANS. TO
READ THEIR PROFILES, PLEASE
TURN THE PAGE.

AND MANY THANKS TO
EVERYONE WHO ENTERED THE
CONTEST.

Theresa Burchett

Theresa is from Southern California, where she has lived all of her life. She is married and is the proud mother of a son and a daughter. Reading is without question a passion of Theresa's—she usually reads a book a day! She has been reading romance for fifteen years, and says that Loveswept is her favorite series because the stories and characters are always interesting. "Years after reading one of your books I could pick it up and remember the characters. Like old friends, they stay in my thoughts," she says.

Theresa's favorite authors include Tami Hoag, Deborah Smith, Sandra Brown, Billie Green, Kay Hooper, Sandra Chastain, and most of all, Iris Johansen.

Christy M. Anderson

Christy got married recently, the day before she mailed her entry to our Treasured Tales III Contest, in fact. Just goes to show that true love can bring good luck as well! Christy is store manager for a men's clothing store as well as an aspiring writer. In her spare time, she likes to work out, loves antiques (especially rings), and of course, loves to read. Christy says that she has been reading romance "since my mother would let me," and her favorite Loveswept authors are Iris Johansen, Jan Hudson, and Fayrene Preston.

Leslie-ann Jones

Leslie-ann was excited to hear that she had won because she says she always enters contests, but never wins. She is a native of Trinidad, and migrated to America with her younger sister to join her mother in 1984. Along with reading (she has 1,327 books, 598 of which are Loveswepts!), Leslie-ann loves sports, animals, collecting stamps, and participating in Carnival. She is also a graduate of Coppin State College, where she earned a B.S. in management science with a minor in computer science.

with the merest whisper of a touch. As fast-paced as a lover's heartbeat, as white-hot as the heat of a candle flame, Fayrene Preston's novel blends daring intrigue and desperate passions, joining an irresistible hero and an unforgettable heroine in a timeless tango of love.

No one touches the heart and tickles the funny bone all at once like Marcia Evanick in **FAMILY FIRST**, LOVESWEPT #779. James Stonewall Carson doesn't look like a grade-school teacher, with his muscled body and shoulders broad enough to carry the world. But there's no mistaking his dedication to the job—or his manly interest in Emmy Lou McNally. Raising six brothers and sisters leaves her no time for dating, but James's sweet talk and fast moves, along with a little help from matchmaking townfolks, pave the way for a delightful courtship. This top-notch read from award-winner Marcia Evanick reveals how tender passion can burn with sizzling heat.

Excitement ripples **UNDER THE COVERS** in Linda Warren's newest LOVESWEPT, #780. He's never been followed by a woman so downright determined, Simon Faro notes with admiration—and more than a touch of curiosity! Detective Jo O'Neal is outrageously persistent in tracking him, even taking on a sassy charade in hopes he'll lead her to criminals she's long been after. Once he proves he's just a reporter nosing around for a scoop, he must convince her to join forces to smoke out the bad guys and set off some fireworks of their own. Linda Warren's steamy romp is a seriously sexy caper that's undeniably fun.

Surrender to the temptation of **SLOW HANDS**, LOVESWEPT #781, by Debra Dixon. Sam Tucker isn't the kind of man to wait for an invitation, not when his mission is to help Clare McGuire learn the joys of losing control! Convinced Sam wants only to change her, the pretty business exec insists she likes her life just as it is—until his kisses brand her with fiery need that echoes her own hunger. Sparring has never been so sweetly seductive as in this delicious treat from Debra Dixon, who entangles a savvy workaholic with a formerly buttoned-down and bottled-up hero determined to show her how to seize the moment.

Happy reading!

With warmest wishes,

Beth de Guzman
Senior Editor

Shauna Summers
Associate Editor

P.S. Watch for these Bantam women's fiction titles coming in February: Tami Hoag's impressive debut hardcover, NIGHT SINS, revealed her to be a masterful spinner of spine-chilling thrills; now, in **GUILTY AS SIN,** she picks up where she left off, delivering non-stop suspense that brings terror to a whole new, even more frightening level. From Teresa Medeiros, nationally bestselling author of FAIREST

Don't miss these extraordinary books
by your favorite Bantam authors

On sale in January:

LION'S BRIDE
by Iris Johansen

SEE HOW THEY RUN
by Bethany Campbell

SCOUNDREL
by Elizabeth Elliott

On sale in February:

GUILTY AS SIN
by Tami Hoag

BREATH OF MAGIC
by Teresa Medeiros

IVY SECRETS
by Jean Stone